praise for courtney summers

"The propulsive, riveting novel that started it all."
—**karen m. mcmanus**, *New York Times* bestselling author of *One of Us Is Lying* and *Two Can Keep a Secret,* on *Cracked Up to Be*

"A modern classic." —**brandy colbert**, award-winning author of *The Revolution of Birdie Randolph* and *Little & Lion,* on *Cracked Up to Be*

"This book is a raw, exposed nerve: all the mess we shouldn't see, shouldn't be, wrapped up in the story of one unforgettable girl." —**rebecca barrow**, author of *This Is What It Feels Like,* on *Cracked Up to Be*

"Absolutely riveting from first page to last."
—**laurie devore**, author of *How to Break a Boy* and *Winner Take All,* on *Cracked Up to Be*

"This book changed me as a reader and as a writer. I could never go back again. After being gutted by a Summers novel, why would anyone want to?" —**nova ren suma**, #1 *New York Times* bestselling author of *The Walls Around Us,* on *Cracked Up to Be*

"A riveting tour de force."
—*Kirkus Reviews* (starred review) on *Sadie*

"Summers excels at slowly unspooling both Sadie's and West's investigations at a measured, tantalizing pace."
—*Booklist* (starred review) on *Sadie*

also by
courtney summers

cracked up to be

courtney summers

WEDNESDAY BOOKS
NEW YORK

Published in the United States by Wednesday Books, an imprint of St. Martin's Publishing Group

www.wednesdaybooks.com

Designed by Anna Gorovoy

The Library of Congress has cataloged the St. Martin's Griffin edition as follows:

Summers, Courtney.
    Cracked up to be / Courtney Summers.—1st ed.
      p. cm.
    ISBN-13: 978-0-312-38369-5
    ISBN-10: 0-312-38369-X
    1. Emotional problems—Fiction.   2. Guilt—Fiction.   3. Interpersonal relations—Fiction.   4. High schools—Fiction.   5. Schools—Fiction.   I. Title.
    PZ7.S95397Cr 2009
    [Fic]—dc22

                                                                      2008031577

ISBN 978-1-250-25697-3 (trade paperback)
ISBN 978-1-4299-4810-4 (ebook)

Our books may be purchased in bulk for promotional, educational, or business use. Please contact your local bookseller or the Macmillan Corporate and Premium Sales Department at 1-800-221-7945, extension 5442, or by email at MacmillanSpecialMarkets@macmillan.com.

First published in the United States by St. Martin's Griffin, an imprint of St. Martin's Publishing Group

First Wednesday Books Edition: February 2020

10 9 8 7 6 5 4 3 2 1

To Lori Thibert,
for inspiring me as a reader,
writer and a person (TG4E),
and to my family, for everything
(and then some)

introduction

The thing with writing is it never feels like it's about the book in front of you—it's about the book you're going to write after that and the book you're going to write after *that*. Being an author is almost never quite arriving at your destination. The stories you finish become no more than stops along the way. The possibilities are endlessly ahead of you and the time to realize them all too short. I look back less and less the longer I'm in this business, but when your publisher decides to reissue your debut over a decade after it first came out, it seems as good a time as any to pause and reflect.

Cracked Up to Be hit shelves December 23, 2008. It was a quiet release; a contemporary story at the height of the paranormal romance—then dystopian—craze. Back then, the YA section of my local chain was no more than two shelves, and after the madness of the holidays, I found copies of my novel there. I took a picture and left, too shy to offer to sign stock. I was twenty-two years old. I was officially an author and I already had another story I wanted to tell the world, and another after that. But *that* seemed entirely dependent on whether or not the world would buy, and hopefully love, my very first book. This was somewhat complicated by the fact its protagonist, Parker Fadley, was determined to make sure everyone hated her.

Some books are a labor of love; *Cracked Up to Be* was a labor of spite. It was my fourth written novel, arriving after three other manuscripts were rejected by literary agents who felt my female main characters were too "unlikable" to sell. I never saw them that way. Complex? Of course. Difficult? Absolutely. The girls I wrote did not always react likably or do likable things, but who does? Doesn't that just mean we're human? The girls I wrote about—and still write about—were often coping with trauma. If they didn't have permission to navigate that space honestly and imperfectly and yes, even, unlikably, then who did?

Oh, right: my male characters.

I shouldn't have been surprised the impossible standards we hold real-life girls to also applied to their fictional counterparts, but I was. And I was angry about it, too. I spent most of my teenage years trying and failing to live up to certain ideals of girlhood at the expense of myself—"sugar and spice and everything nice"—and being able to express that pressure through my work was a lifeline. So when I was told that expression was a little too off-putting to be widely read, well . . . it sounded like a challenge to me.

Parker Fadley is a girl who doesn't quite know how to live up to those ideals, either, and her solution is perfection. "I get caught up in outcomes," she confesses at one point. "I convince myself they're truths. No one will notice how wrong you are if everything you do ends up right." When she fails to be the perfect girl, she throws everything she's got into being the perfect mess and her spectacular unraveling is many things—least of all likable.

The act of writing makes me a better writer. I give my

books everything I have when I write them, so I'm always assured they're the best I could offer readers at the time. Because of this, my body of work exists as both a point of pride and a measure of my growth.

Cracked Up to Be marks a younger Courtney Summers and Parker Fadley is one of the most teenaged characters you'll find in one of my books. The crackling energy of her stream-of-consciousness narrative, and the razor-sharp dialogue, surprises and delights me when I revisit it. The bravado driving her obnoxious sense of humor and cutting, often thoughtless retorts fails to conceal a greater vulnerability that makes me very sad in turn. *Love me in spite of me,* Parker is constantly unconsciously begging the people in her life.

Cracked Up to Be had its champions from the outset, primarily my editor and then-agent—it was a first book for all of us. They believed in Parker's story enough to bring it to the public and I will always be grateful to them for that. But *Cracked Up to Be* did not have the kind of pre- and postpublication reception that would lead me to believe I'd be preparing an introduction for its reissue a dozen years later. In fact, its first trade review tore Parker's salt-of-the-earth campaign to shreds (leaving me impervious to all future trade reviews) and I vividly remember staring at Goodreads and thinking it could easily go either way. Not being immediately recognized as a critically brilliant, instant classic or being positioned or marketed to become the next great commercial blockbuster meant the most I could hope for was its resonance with the readers who did pick it up. And I hoped for that, so much.

Happily, those readers found Parker. And they didn't love her in spite of her. They loved her *because* of her. *Cracked Up to Be* remains one of my most cherished books among the girls and women who have read it and their enduring support has meant the world to me over the course of my career.

Throughout the years, the countless emails and messages I've received have helped me better understand *why* Parker's story means so much to them. I've realized that loving and forgiving Parker has become a way for them to love and forgive themselves. It makes sense—that was one of the reasons I wrote it for me, too.

(That, and the spite.)

There's another reason I don't often look back when it comes to writing—it seems unnecessary because you're never as far from those stops along the way as you might think. It's been more than ten years, and Parker Fadley is still the backbone of all my characters who have followed. Without her, there would be no Regina, no Eddie, no Sloane, no Romy, and no Sadie—or the girl after that, or the girl after that . . . which is fitting, really. I don't think Parker would have it any other way.

Neither would I.

Courtney Summers
April 2019

cracked
up to be

one

Imagine four years.

Four years, two suicides, one death, one rape, two pregnancies (one abortion), three overdoses, countless drunken antics, pantsings, spilled food, theft, fights, broken limbs, turf wars—every day, a turf war—six months until graduation and no one gets a medal when they get out. But everything you do here counts.

High school.

"No, seriously, Jules, just feel around in there and tell me if you have one—"

"Fuck off, Chris—"

"And tell me where it is, the *exact* location."

"You're disgusting!"

"Hey, Parker!"

He reaches out and grabs me by the shoulder. I shrug, shrug, shrug him off.

"Fuck off, Chris."

He's been on about the G-spot for, like, a week.

"Don't fail me now, Parker. Where is it?"

"*Cosmo,* December '94. The Sex Issue. Came with a map and everything."

"Hell yes! I knew I could count on you." He points at me, grinning, and then the grin falters and he says, "Wait. You bullshitting me?"

I make him wait for the answer because I'm bullshitting him.

"Chris, I respect you too much to do that."

"That's so sweet. You look good today, Parker."

"You bullshitting me?"

"I respect *you* too much to do that."

I look like shit today for a variety of reasons, but let's start with the muddy running shoes on my feet. Running shoes are expressly forbidden to wear with the school uniform, but damned if I know where my dress shoes disappeared to between now and yesterday. And then there's my uniform skirt, which has a mustard stain on the front because I can't do something simple like make a sandwich for lunch without screwing it up. I plucked my rumpled polo shirt from my bedroom floor and I guess I could've brushed my hair if I'd wanted to forgo the bus ride and walk all ten miles to school, but supposedly if I miss any more classes I could maybe not graduate, and if I have to spend another year in this concrete block—

"Shoes, Parker!"

Principal Henley's got her arms crossed and her eyebrows up. I bring my hands together like I'm appealing to God. I might as well be.

"One day only, Mrs. Henley. See, I got up really late and I couldn't find my dress shoes and I was *so* worried about getting here on time—"

"And the hair—"

"Can be brushed," I say, smoothing my hand over the tangles.

"You're due at the guidance office in five minutes."

"Oh, joy," I say. Her eyes flash and I smile. "No, really."

Her eyebrows go down. It's good, but not as good as when I got away with everything. I elbow my way through a mass of people to get to my locker because there's something immensely satisfying about the toughest part of my arm connecting with the softest part of everyone else. A shapely embodiment of a female Satan appears on the horizon, flipping her long blond hair over her shoulder as she commands the attention of her many underlings. My former underlings.

Becky Halprin.

"—I just bluffed my way through it," she's saying as I pass. "Hey, Parker?"

I half turn. "What?"

"Did you get that essay finished for Lerner?"

Shit.

"That was due today?"

Becky stares at me.

"You only had the whole weekend."

I open my locker. "Why do you sound surprised?"

"Bet you fifty bucks you're fucked."

"You're on," I say. "I can do a lot with fifty bucks."

She laughs and heads wherever she's heading. Cheerleading practice, maybe. No. It's too early, and anyway, I don't care.

Lerner's essay.

I grab my planner and flip through it until I find the page with *FRIDAY* and *HOMEWORK* scrawled messily at the top but nothing underneath. Great. The bell rings. Guidance office.

Shit.

I grab my brush, slam my locker shut and race against the flow of students heading to their respective homerooms. I reach the office while the bell's still ringing. I take a minute to catch my breath, stalling, because Ms. Grey would cream herself if she thought I actually made the effort to be on time and I don't like giving people false hope. I count to ten and run a brush through my hair. One. Two. Three. Ten. Again. A few minutes go by. A few more.

When I finally decide to enter the office, I'm still brushing my hair.

It's not meant to be insolent—it's *not* insolent—but the thing is, I can't stop. My hair looks fine, but I just stand there brushing it in front of Grey, who sits at her desk looking all devastated, like I'm mocking her somehow.

Sorry, I can't stop, I want to say, but I don't. I don't think I'm really sorry about it, either, but she should know this isn't some kind of slam at her for making my life a little more inconvenient than it already is. If it was, I'd be a lot more creative about it.

I sit down across from her and run the brush through my hair a few more times.

"You're late," she finally manages.

My hand relaxes. I lower the brush and rest it in my lap. Grey looks like a bird, a dead-eyed sparrow, and if I had her job, I'd want to kill myself. It's not like well-adjusted people ever come into the guidance office. You get either the crazy underachievers or the crazy overachievers and both come with their own depressing set of problems.

I don't know. I'd just want to kill myself if I was her, that's all.

"Yeah," I say. "So we'd better get on with it, huh?"

"Right." She clasps her hands together. "You already know this, but I think it bears repeating: no cutting, no missed days, no exceptions. You *will* complete your homework and you *will* hand it in when it's due. Off-campus lunch privileges are suspended until you can prove to us that you're trustworthy again and—"

"But what if I wake up one morning and I can't stop vomiting or I'm hemorrhaging or something? Do I still have to go to school?"

She blinks. "What?"

"What if I'm really sick? What do I do then?"

"A parent would have to call in for you. Otherwise you'll receive a warning—"

"Right." I nod and start chewing my thumbnail. "Okay."

She clears her throat.

"On Friday, you'll meet me here and we'll talk about any troubles you might have had throughout the week, the progress you've made both in and out of school, and—"

"But what if I miss some assignments, though? I've gone so long just not doing them, I think it's kind of unfair to expect me to get back on the ball right away. You know what I think, Ms. Grey? I think I should get a grace period."

She leans across the desk, her dead eyes showing a rare sign of life. It freaks me out so much I have to look away.

"This *is* your grace period, Parker."

Then I have to run all the way to homeroom. Mr. Bradley makes a point to glare at me when he marks down my attendance because they all must have gotten the Tough Love memo over the weekend. I pause at Chris's desk and tap my fingers along the wood until he looks up from the math homework he's scrambling to finish.

"Becky knows where it is."

He laughs. "Becky? You're talking to her now?"

"Yeah. About G-spots. At length. She's an expert."

"Okay." His pale blue eyes twinkle. "Send her up."

I wink at him and head to the desk at the back of the room, where Becky's alternately painting her nails and the cover of her binder with sparkly red polish. A nail here, a red heart there. I slide into the seat next to hers and I don't waste time.

"Chris wants you."

Her head whips up.

"Chris wants *me*?"

"Yeah. Go see."

She looks from me to him to me again, to him, to me, and she grins. Chris is popular, cute, all dimples. He wears his uniform shirt a size too small because it makes his muscles look bigger than they actually are and he's never wanted Becky before.

"Thanks," she whispers, standing.

She squares her shoulders and walks up the aisle as sexily she can, which is not very sexy at all. As soon as her back is to me, I grab her binder and flip through it, carefully avoiding the drying polish decorating the front. It's so beautifully organized, I find Lerner's essay before Becky even gets to Chris.

We were supposed to write about patriarchy and *Beowulf*. I had no idea we even read *Beowulf*, but I'm resigned to the fact I can't bullshit my way through this essay as effortlessly as Becky probably has, and since I'm pretty confident she can do it just as effortlessly again, I rip it from her binder.

It's my essay now.

"He's disgusting," Becky says when she comes back.

The funny thing is, she won't even notice the essay's missing until Lerner's class and even then she won't suspect me, because I may have done a lot of stupid things in the last year, but that doesn't mean I'm an *essay thief*. People are kind of stupid like that when they think you're tragic. You get away with a lot even after you're caught.

"You obviously like disgusting," I tell her.

She smiles this big blond smile.

"He asked me out for Friday, but I wanted to make sure it's okay with you first."

Right.

"Screw him, Becky. I don't care."

"Parker—"

"Becky, really. I don't want to hear it. You're dull."

She rolls her eyes. "For five seconds you almost seemed human."

"Five whole seconds, huh? That's an improvement. Tell Grey; she'll love that."

The bell rings and Becky lunges out of her seat. Chris waits for no one.

"Becky," I call after her. She turns. "I hope you have that fifty on you. I'll need it for after school."

I copy her essay during history, unnecessarily exerting myself with a little creative rewriting so it sounds authentically Parker.

After history, I run into the new kid.

The bell has rung, the halls are filtering out and when I spot him, this new kid, he's doing that confused stumble around the halls that makes it painfully obvious he has no idea where he is. He's got brown hair that sort of hangs into his brown eyes and I stare at him when I pass, because new kids generally can't handle eye contact and I find that amusing. He looks about eighteen and I bet his parents are assholes to do whatever it is they did that he had to transfer in the middle of senior year.

"Hey . . . hey, you—girl!"

I turn slowly, debating. Do I make this easy on him or do I make it hard?

A good person would make it easy.

I decide to start with mocking and work my way up.

"Hey . . . hey, you—New Kid!"

He takes it well.

"Uh, yeah. Hi," he says. "Maybe you could help me?"

"I'm late for class."

"That makes two of us." He smiles. "Of course, you have

an advantage in that you probably know where class is. Could you tell me where Mr. Norton's room is?"

"Sorry, New Kid. Can't. I'm late."

"Oh, come on. You have time—"

"No. I have no time."

Pause, pause, pause. We stare at each other for a good minute.

"You're just standing there," he finally splutters. "How can you have time for *that* but not enough time to tell me how to get to Mr. Norton's room?"

I give him my most winning smile, shrug and resume the walk to *my* next class.

Art.

"Are they all like you around here?"

I wave over my shoulder, but I don't stop.

Norton says he's going to tell on me for being late. Henley and Grey will get the notice and I'll have to discuss it on Friday. *Why were you late, Parker? What did you think that would accomplish, Parker?* And then the tough question. *What destructive behaviors were you engaging in for the five minutes you weren't in class, Parker?*

I'm going to tell them I'm on my period.

Anyway, I have two classes with Chris and this is one of them. We sit next to each other because his last name starts with *E* and mine starts with *F*. Ellory and Fadley, Winter Ball King and Queen three years running.

I can't stand being around him, but I fake it pretty well.

"You're late," Chris says. We're working with charcoal today. He passes me a pencil and a sheet of paper. "Where were you?"

"If I told you, I'd only disappoint you."

"Jesus, Parker."

I start working on a charcoal blob. Abstract charcoal. Whatever. The black flakes off the pencil tip, making a nice mess of my fingers pretty quickly. Then I smudge until my master-piece is ruined. I bet Norton will report that, too, like I didn't *try*, even though it's art, where no one should be able to tell if you're trying or not.

The stupid thing is, I like art. I mean, it's okay.

"Oh, Jesus yourself and take a joke," I tell him. "There's a new kid. He asked me directions. It took a couple min-utes."

"Oh." He sounds relieved. "Hey, your hair looks nice all brushed like that."

"Took you long enough to notice. It was brushed in home-room."

"I've got a date with Becky for Friday."

"Chris and Becky," I say thoughtfully. I try it again in Movie Announcer Voice: "Chris and Becky. *Presenting Chris and Becky* . . ."

He stares. "What?"

"It doesn't sound right," I declare. "There's no ring to it."

"Yeah, well, you broke up with me."

"I know; I was there. And that has nothing to do with how stupid your names sound together." I try it again: "Chris, Becky, Becky, Chris . . ."

He stares some more.

"Seriously, there's a new kid? You're not drunk?"

"No, I'm on my period."

Enter New Kid. The door swings open and he's flushed and out of breath like he ran all the way here. Everyone gets quiet—fresh meat—and Norton *harrumphs*.

"Better late than never. Gardner, I presume?"

"Yes, sir," Gardner mumbles. "I got lost."

"Late slip?"

Gardner looks like he can't believe it. "I'm *new*."

"Thank you for that, Gardner. Take a seat over there, help yourself to some charcoal and paper and get to work." Norton's

such a hard-ass. He reminds me of George C. Scott sometimes. "I expect you to be on time tomorrow."

"That's not the guy you gave directions to, is it?" Chris
asks.

"I didn't say I *gave* him directions; I said he asked me for
them."

"Christ, Parker, you're a real bitch sometimes."

Gardner skulks over to the table next to ours, sets up and
starts drawing. I stare at him until he feels it and looks my
way. His eyes widen and he points his charcoal pencil at me
accusingly.

"You," he says. "You're in this class?"

I smile. "Hi. I'm Parker Fadley."

Chris reaches past me, extending his hand.

"Ignore her. I'm Chris Ellory. Welcome to St. Peter's."

"Thanks," Gardner says, looking relieved that they're not
all like me around here. He and Chris shake hands. "Jake
Gardner. Nice to meet you."

Now that I've heard his name, I'm doomed to remember it.
Just more useless information taking up brain space that could
be better served for more important things like . . . stuff. Jake
and Chris talk through art and discover they have so much
in common it's amazing. Like, They Could Be Boyfriends If
They Didn't Like Vaginas So Much Amazing.

By the time the period is over, my charcoal blob has eaten
all the white space but for one solitary speck to the lower left
side of my paper. When Norton does his rounds, he leans
over my shoulder and, in his best George C. Scott, says,
"I like it." Then he glances at Chris's halfhearted elm and
goes, "It's always trees with you! How many times do I have
to tell you to *think outside the tree,* Ellory?" And I laugh so
hard I cry a little.

Then the bell goes off again. The bell goes off too much.

We eke our way out of the room and Chris turns to Jake

and says, "We're gonna check out the fast-food strip for lunch. Wanna come?"

"Sure," Jake says.

"How about it, Parker?" Chris asks me. Then he brings his hands to his mouth in mock horror. "Oops, forgot. You're not allowed off grounds for lunch anymore!"

I roll my eyes.

He says something else, but I don't hear it because I'm gone. I drop my things at my locker and search out a spot in school that isn't around people, but there are none and that's when I notice that the halls are way too crowded.

There are bodies everywhere.

At first I do okay. I hover by the drinking fountain and try to look like I've got somewhere to be. Then I start hearing this sound, like this sighing, no—not sighing. *Breathing.* Everyone breathing. I can hear the people around me sucking up all the fresh air, leaving nothing for me.

My chest tightens and I can't breathe.

"I can't breathe."

I scare the hell out of the school nurse. He darts up from his chair and makes a big fuss while I try to explain the problem.

"I can't breathe. The air in here is too stale. . . . No, my chest feels fine. Yes, I can feel my left arm. . . . Make them open some windows; they're using up all the air. . . ."

He doesn't get it, but he directs me to a cot at the back of the room anyway. No one else is sick today, so I get a little peace and quiet. I lie on my back and scan the shelves across the room for a bottle of ipecac, but no such luck.

I close my eyes.

When I open them again, it's last period and I'm in English and Becky is freaking out and flipping through her binder while Lerner looks on. I don't know what she's so worried about; she's golden. She never misses an essay and Lerner likes her. He's even saying, "No worries, Halprin, just get it to me by the end of the week—"

"But you don't understand, sir; I *did* the essay! I *had* it! It was *here!*"

"I'm sure it will turn up," he tells her soothingly. "Just make sure you hand it in by Friday. . . ."

Becky looks like she's going to cry. Lerner moves on to me.

"I don't even have to ask, do I, Fadley?"

Lerner likes me, too. Not as much as he used to. What I like best about Lerner is he's been teaching so long, he doesn't waste time. He readjusted his expectations of me immediately after the first time I got wasted and fell out of my chair in class.

"I think you should," I say, smiling. "Go on, ask."

His mustache twitches. "Well, I'm afraid to now."

Becky's mouth drops open as I make a show out of taking the essay from my binder and handing it to Lerner. He stares at it, and then me, and for a second I wonder if he knows it's Becky's. But then he tucks it away with the other papers he's collected and it's good. Only I hope he doesn't do any expectation readjusting after this because then I'll have to disappoint him.

Becky gapes at me, still teary eyed.

"When the fuck did you do that essay?"

"History, lunch. I'll take my fifty dollars now, please."

"I was joking, Parker. The bet was a *joke.*"

But I won't let it be a joke, so when the last bell, finally, mercifully, *rings,* I chase after her down the hall, screaming her name.

"Becky! Hey, Becky! *Becky Halprin!*"

She pauses, stuck. At one end of the hall, her crew—my old crew—and at the other end, me. She thinks about it for a minute, sighs and heads in my direction.

"What?"

"What time's your date with Chris on Friday?"

She blushes.

"He's picking me up at six."

"Do you still have that pink sweater? The one that's supertight across the chest? You should wear that, he'd like it." She looks all disgusted because she's too stupid to realize I'm helping her out.

"Uh." She blinks. "Okay. Thanks. I think."

"No problem." I pause. "Hey, if *you'd* won the bet, would it still have been a joke?"

"Becky, come *on*," someone whines behind us. I glance down the hall. Sandra Morrison is tapping her foot impatiently and giving me a look of utter disdain, which is pretty amazing considering she wouldn't have dared to do it when *I* was the one leading her around by the nose. Becky sighs and briefly closes her eyes before reaching into her book bag, finding her wallet and pulling out a few crisp bills.

"Thanks," I tell her as she hands them to me. "I hope your essay turns up."

She looks touched, like I mean it.

"I do, too. You know, Tori quit the squad. There's a position available."

I snort. "Like I'd ever let you captain me."

Her mouth drops open, but I don't give her the chance to say anything back. I walk away, get my things out of my locker and head home. I'm tired of being around people my age, so I skip the bus, make the short walk to the city's main street and hail a cab.

I can afford it now.

two

"V-I-C-T-O-R-Y!
"HIT 'EM LOW AND HIT 'EM HIGH!
"V-I-C-T-O-R-Y!
"LET'S GO, JACKALS! WIN OR DIE!
"V-I-C-T-O-R-Y!"

Grey says I'm not allowed to spend lunch period in the nurse's office anymore because no one will take me seriously should the time ever come that I actually *can't* breathe, so I go to the gym and sit in on cheerleading practice instead. It's a pretty low-key affair. The squad takes up the far side of the court and Chris, his buddies and his new puppy, Jake, play a game of twenty-one on the opposite end.

It's sort of like old times except I'm not on top of the pyramid anymore. It was a relief for everyone the day I quit the squad. Jessie had been gone for a while. On a number of occasions I'd miscalculated how many shots of vodka you could down without going to class completely wasted, and anyway, I hadn't been showing up for practice for ages, and seeing as I was captain and everything . . .

Becky made herself cry so it looked like she actually cared about my well-being, like she was only taking over captaining duties *super*reluctantly, but because her mascara wasn't waterproof she wound up looking so ridiculous I laughed in her face in front of the whole squad. What was supposed to be a superficially touching moment for the girls and me didn't end very well.

In fact, they hate me now.

I broke up with Chris pretty shortly after that.

"V-I-C-T-O-R-Y!"

Chris emerges champion of twenty-one and the boys start an impromptu mini-game, except for Jake, who doesn't know I know he's been watching me every chance he gets, these "subtle" glances out the corners of his eyes. He casually removes himself from the game and makes his way up the bleachers. Our impending encounter has already left me exhausted, but at least I look better today than I did Monday. Dress shoes on feet (they were under the bed), clean skirt and shirt. My hair's brushed and in a tight ponytail at the back of my head. I slept well last night.

He sits down beside me. "We got off on the wrong foot."

"Did we?" I inhale. "Ew. I hope you're going to shower before class."

"Or maybe there is no right foot with you."

Silence. Jake shifts, laughs nervously and runs a hand through his hair. People always get uncomfortable when I decide to shut up. You'd think it'd be the opposite, but no.

After a couple of minutes, he bravely soldiers on:

"Chris told me I had better things to do than talk to you, but I kind of wanted to do it anyway."

Oh, Chris. I owe him a thousand apologies, but I don't have the time and he doesn't want to hear them. Also, I'm not sorry.

"He said that because he's not over me," I explain.

"Oh." Jake nods. After a beat, his eyes get comically wide. *"Oh."*

"Yeah."

I stand and stretch and he does the same, shifting some more. I focus my attention on the cheerleaders. Becky is in her element now that she's captain. She wants to coach professionally someday and the reality is she could do far worse and not much better. She shouts the girls into a ragged formation. We're not going to win any awards this year. I'm gone, Tori's gone and Jessie won't be back for who knows how long.

"Anyway," Jake says. I turn back to him. "I just wanted to start over on a good note, that's all."

I have to put this poor guy out of his misery.

"Look, Jake, I'm not in the market for—" I almost say *a boyfriend,* which is true, but this is even truer: "People."

"The-that's presumptuous of you," he stutters because he hears the *boyfriend* of it anyway, like I knew he would. "I . . . I'm not—"

"Aren't you?" I study him. I'm really not that presumptuous, but I need to kill this conversation. "Why else would you want to talk to me?"

"I was giving you a chance to redeem yourself for being such a bitch on Monday," he says, turning red all over. What a saint. "I thought I'd be nice to you—"

"And get into my pants in the process, right?"

"HIT 'EM LOW AND HIT 'EM HIGH!"

He's completely gobsmacked. Maybe they don't talk so forward wherever he came from. And I've no doubt he's probably a nice guy who poses no immediate threat to my hymen—if I still had one—but I meant what I said. I'm not in the market for people.

I want to be alone.

So I leave Jake on the bleachers.

After math, I'm due at the guidance office for my first of many sessions where I talk about my adventures on the straight and narrow and how I *feel* about it. Grey's in a cheerful mood when I sit across from her. Cheerful for Grey, anyway.

"I'm glad you showed up," she says. "Principal Henley and I had a bet on whether or not you'd skip and now I'm twenty dollars richer."

"She underestimates how much I want to graduate," I say.

"Well, I didn't." Grey smiles. "Let's get started. I want you to be open with me, Parker."

I take a deep breath. It smells suspiciously like bullshit in here.

"Open?" I repeat.

"Open. This is your space. Feel free to say anything. You have my word it won't leave the room. I want you to trust me. In learning to trust me, I learn to trust you, and from that trust we go forward. You get your life back and you graduate a person everyone can be proud of."

She looks over a piece of paper in front of her. I'm betting it's some kind of Parker Tally Sheet.

"You did well this week, mostly," she says.

It's funny—I think I'd actually rather be learning right now.

"I guess."

"You've done most of your homework. Good. Next week try for all of it, okay? Mrs. Jones informed me she's willing to be lenient about math since you've managed to get behind an entire unit, but that's not indefinite. I thought that was generous of her."

"Oh yes." I nod. "Very."

We get quiet. Grey's office is such a pit. There are no windows in here and some dumb ass thought fluorescent lights would be a great way to compensate. If anyone comes in here ready to die, they probably leave feeling that way, too.

"What are you thinking about, Parker?"

I'm thinking about Becky and Chris and how they've been making eyes at each other all day, and how in third period I realized by this time tomorrow both of us will have kissed him and how if they fall for each other, that means I'm replaceable. If I'm replaceable, if I step back and put something in the space where I was, I can probably get to be alone faster than I already am. Like, Becky and Chris get together and some new girl joins the squad and they forget about me. Next, I find someone who fucked up worse than I did, like some student prostitute who cuts herself, and that takes care of Henley and Grey and then—maybe I can convince my parents they need a puppy.

"I'm not thinking about anything."

"Fine." She purses her lips. "Let's get back to the week. There were a few glitches. The nurse's office. I don't know what that was about. And you were late for Mr. Norton's class on Monday. Mind telling me why?"

"I ran into the new kid. Jake something. He needed directions."

"Oh." She seems relieved. "So you weren't—"

"Don't worry, Ms. Grey. I wasn't drinking, smoking, toking or snorting in school. I keep the recreational drug use at home where it belongs."

"Parker," she warns.

I lean back and stare at the ceiling. The first time I was in this office was the last time I was drunk at school. I was slumped over in the very chair I'm sitting in now and Henley and Grey discussed my "situation" right in front of me, like there was no way I could follow what they were saying or remember any of it in the morning, but I did.

This is sad; this is so sad. . . .

"So," she says.

"So."

"So . . . ?"

She's superineffectual. I decide to mess with her.

"Actually, I kind of liked getting back into the swing of things. Becky even offered me a position on the squad and that was *so* nice. Handing in my homework, talking to that Jake guy—it almost felt . . ." I insert a carefully calculated pause here. "Never mind; it's stupid."

"No, no." She leans forward eagerly. "You can trust me, Parker."

I stare at my hands.

"It almost felt like . . . *before*."

Grey loves it. She almost falls out of her chair; that's how convincing I am.

That's great, Parker; that's wonderful! See? We'll get you back yet! And then I clam up. *No, it's stupid. You're wrong. It's stupid. Never mind.* Because there's no qualifying exam to be a high school guidance counselor. All you have to do is watch a bunch of cheesy movies about troubled teens and take notes. This is how Grey expects the meeting to go down and I'm giving it to her because it might get me out of here faster or, at the very least, end this discussion.

"No, it's stupid," I repeat robotically.

"No, it isn't. It's not stupid. *Never* think it is."

I offer a cautious smile. "Thanks."

She creams herself.

The bell rings. I make a beeline for the door.

"Parker?"

I don't turn, just wait.

"That was really good," she says. "You know, I think there's a lot more hope for you than *you* think there is."

I roll my eyes.

"Thanks, Ms. G."

Becky accosts me as soon as I step into the hall, waving a sheet of paper in my face.

"Here," she says, as I take it. "I copied down homework for you. Lerner had a headache so he told us to read 'The Yellow Wallpaper' again—"

"We read it before?"

"Yeah, in ninth grade. Anyway, he wants us to write a thousand words on how we relate to the story now, as seniors, compared to how we related to it as freshmen. It's pretty half-assed, but like I said, he had a headache."

"'The Yellow Wallpaper' is the one where the chick goes insane and starts humping the wall at the end, right?"

She stares. "You might wanna reread it again to be safe."

Pfft. "We'll see. Ready for your date tonight?"

"Yeah, got my pink sweater dry-cleaned and everything," she says, and then she puts on her fake-interested face. "How'd your meeting with Grey go?"

"It's six o'clock, right? The date?" I ask. She nods. "Look, I've got to go. I don't want to miss the bus."

On the ride home, I pass the time imagining their date. Chris will take Becky somewhere predictable and nice, even though he could take her Dumpster diving and she'd be happy because she's wanted him so long, and he'll spend the whole time trying desperately hard not to stare at her breasts, because that G-spot stuff is all bravado, but by the end of the night he'll be feeling her up, telling her she's pretty, *the prettiest,* and she'll blush and say, *Oh, Chris,* and they'll make another date and they'll fall in love and she'll be a cheerleading coach and he'll be an heir and they'll have two-point-five kids and, and, and . . .

"I think we should get a dog."

It's one of my better entrances. Dad lowers the paper and Mom drops the potato she's peeling over the sink and they look at me like I'm certifiable, but I'd rather be certifiable than perpetually boring, which is my parents in a nutshell. If I had to own up to resembling either one of them, it'd be my dad. We both have blond hair and sharp features. Mom's less sharp, more Pillsbury.

"A dog?" Mom says, retrieving the potato. "You think we should get a dog?"

"That's what I said."

Dad returns to the paper. "I've always wanted a dog."

"Well, a puppy actually," I say.

"I've always wanted a puppy," he amends. "They turn into dogs."

"What?" Mom demands, turning to him. "What's that supposed to mean? We're getting a puppy, just like that?"

"No, not just like *that*. We'd have to talk about it more. Figure out the logistics." He glances at Mom. "It wouldn't be so terrible, would it? Having a dog?"

She turns to me.

"Where did this come from, Parker? You don't want a dog."

"Yes, I do! Ms. Grey said it would be good for me to— to . . ." I chew my lip and start making faces that obviously indicate I'm in the process of lying, but my parents hate believing I do that. Lie. "She said it would be a good learning experience for me. By learning to nurture a puppy into a healthy dog I could . . . in turn . . . learn to nurture myself again! *And* I did all my homework this week, so I'd say I've earned it."

"You couldn't start out with a goldfish?"

"Goldfish die at the drop of a hat, Mom. It could die of completely natural causes after two weeks and I might think it was something *I* did and I wouldn't be able to live with myself. Puppies are harder to kill and more challenging to take care of and I'm pretty sure that's the point."

Mom and Dad exchange a lo-ng look.

"We'll have to talk about it," Dad says, which means we're getting a dog.

"Great. You two do that and call me when dinner's ready. I'll be in my room."

"But don't you want to tell us about the rest of your—"

I'm a bad daughter. I don't go to my room at first; I hang back in the hall and listen. Mom and Dad are quiet for a little bit and then Mom goes, "Did you find that as oddly encouraging as I did?"

And Dad goes, "Yeah. She hasn't really talked to us in a long time."

"You think her guidance counselor really thinks she should get a dog?"

"It could be a lie."

"And if it is?"

"We can check. But look, if she *is* lying it's because she wants a dog. It's not like she's lying about where she's been and who she's been with. . . ."

My dad, the softie.

"And that makes it okay?"

"No, but maybe a dog could foster some kind of . . . sense of responsibility and . . . discourage her recklessness. . . ."

"So we should get a dog? That's what you're saying?"

"Who knows? But she talked to us, Lara. She asked us for something we can give her."

"It would be nice to feel like we were doing something." Quiet. Mom clears her throat. "Now come over here and taste this and tell me if it's awful. . . ."

I check out at dinnertime. I mean, I'm there and I'm eating, but I spend the meal staring into space, nodding my head every time it's clear my parents are talking to me and sometimes when it isn't. When our plates are empty and we fall into that awkward silence that happens between digesting and clearing the table, I come back to myself.

"May I please go for a walk?"

It's a big question because I have a curfew now, but my parents' spines are so pliable I don't think it'll be a problem. Mom and Dad exchange a nervous glance and have a telepathic conversation about it. I hear every word.

Do we let her out? It's past curfew.

True, but look at that—at least she asked!

I know! I can hardly believe it!

She could have just sneaked out, but she asked!

I know! We're good parents!

"What time will you be back?" Dad asks.

"What time is it now?"

"It's seven."

"Within the hour, I guess."

"Where are you going?"

"It's just a walk." I make sure to look them both in the eyes. "That's it."

"Sure . . . ," Mom says slowly, staring at Dad, who nods slightly. "That would be fine. Thank you for asking, Parker."

I'm out of the house quick in case they change their minds. It's dark out, but I have a Mini Maglite attached to my key ring, so I'm not worried. It feels nice having the streets to myself. Every so often I hear the sound of cars in the distance navigating some faraway road.

Chris lives two blocks from me, in the nicest house on the nicest piece of property in all of Corby, Connecticut, and I'm sure he's still out with Becky and no doubt his parents are at the country club. When his house comes into view, I walk up the gravel driveway casually, so if any of the neighbors happen to look out their windows I'm only here for a visit. Nothing unusual.

I bypass the front door and edge my way around the house, maneuvering past shriveled flower beds and tacky lawn ornaments until I find myself in the backyard, facing the woods

behind the house. These woods never change. The pine trees
stand tall and separate, illuminated by the light of some far-
off source. When I come here, it always takes me a while to
get my bearings, but I can't afford to do that tonight because
I promised my parents I'd be home within the hour and I'm
not wearing a watch.

I trudge into the trees and pull out my Mini Maglite. One
step, two steps, ten steps, twenty, twenty-five steps. I turn
the flashlight on. A feeble, yellow light reveals a small strip
of ground laden with pine needles.

It was around here . . .

And then, without fail, I hear the music from that night,
like I always do when I come out here. A heavy bass line and
an earsplitting drumbeat winds its way into the woods from
Chris's open bedroom window, where he likes to mount the
speakers of his sound system for optimal noise blaring into
the neighborhood. And then there's splashing sounds coming from the pool and everyone's laughing and talking and
shrieking and having a good time.

His parties are the best.

I stick the flashlight in my mouth, get down on my hands
and knees and start pushing aside pine needles. Five minutes
later, my throat hitches. I rip the flashlight from my mouth,
scramble backward and throw up.

Fuck.

I wipe my mouth, force myself to my feet, move past the
puddle of vomit and get back to work. I don't know what I
think I'll find out here, but I stay on the ground for a while
anyway, searching, until I know the hour's gone and I'm late
and I'd better go. I don't want Chris to come back and see
me here and ask me what I'm doing.

Finding the bracelet that time was just a fluke, Parker,
you idiot.

three

Jake's a rather tenacious young man. Monday starts with him waiting for me by my locker, and I'm really not in the mood for it because I might have a hangover.

Okay, that's not true. I'm kind of in the mood for it because it *is* vaguely intriguing. I have clearly charmed the guy out of his mind.

"You're in my way." I nudge him aside. I think Grey knows I'm hungover. She gave me this extralong look when we passed in the hall earlier, and that's never good. I grab my history books and slam my locker shut, which makes the bad headache I'm nursing worse. Like that, my vague state of intrigue fades. "What do you want, Jake?"

"In your pants." He turns red and cringes. "I mean, I don't want into your pants. And I didn't. I'm not interested in you."

"Okay." I bite the inside of my cheek to keep from laughing. "Thanks for that."

I head for homeroom, but Jake expects more apparently, because he follows after me.

"That's it? That's all you're going to say?"

"You don't want in my pants. Duly noted."

A couple passing freshmen give us startled looks.

"Look, I was just trying to be nice to you and—"

"Give me the chance to redeem myself; I know," I say. "When you were obsessing over our conversation this weekend, did you take a moment to appreciate what a jerk kind of thing that is to say?"

"I offended *you*?"

"Not likely. I just thought you'd want to know how it made you sound. You're obviously one of those people who really care about what other people think of you."

"*What?*"

I stop; he stops.

"I didn't really think you wanted in my pants, Jake, but if you spent the whole weekend waiting for today just so you could clear that up, you have some issues."

"*I* have issues?"

"There. Admitting you have a problem is half the battle."

"You know, you're not half as clever as you think you are."

"This still makes me a lot cleverer than you."

We arrive at homeroom. Perfect timing. I get to leave Jake sputtering in the doorway. It's almost worth being early for that alone.

The room is only half-full and Becky is nowhere to be found, but Chris is seated in the middle row, working on his homework. He's almost as bad as I am, if not for the fact that he usually gets it done.

"Uh-oh," he says, looking up as I approach. "I know that face."

"Do you ever do your homework at home?"

"About half." He finishes up some English and I sit down beside him for the hell of it. He closes his book. "You're hung-over."

"I have a hungover face?"

"It's subtle, but it's there." It's stuff like this that makes me glad we broke up. He pauses. "You want to talk about it?"

"I think my face says it all. How was your date with Becky?"

He forces a smile. The right corner of his mouth starts twitching.

"Good," he says, in a voice that belies the word. "It was good."

"Uh-oh, I know *that* face."

He groans and leans back in his seat. "Becky's a great girl—"

I clutch my heart. "There's not going to be a second date!"

"Did I say that?"

"Yeah, when you called her a *great girl*." This poses a problem. Becky's supposed to be my replacement, or at the very least they could distract each other from me for a while. I'll have to lie, but it's for a worthwhile cause. "She *is* a great girl. You'd be an idiot if you let her go."

"Parker, you hate Becky. And you're taking an unusual interest in my date with her. Jealous?" I laugh and he gives me this look. "No, really. Why do you care? And why are you hungover?"

I put on my most Obnoxious Teacher Talking to a Really, Really Stupid Student voice.

"Well, Chris, sometimes when someone overindulges—"

"You do know that Becky and I are supposed to report any kind of behavior like this to Grey and Henley?"

"That's funny. Tell me another."

"It's not a joke."

"It was because she's not me, isn't it? That's why it didn't work out, huh? Becky's a *great girl,* but she's no Parker Fadley. It's okay. I understand. I *am* pretty awesome."

"Fuck you."

"Fuck you, too. And if you tell Henley or Grey, I'll kick your ass."

He snorts. "Oh, really?"

"Yeah, and I'll probably get away with it, because I'm a girl. Make sure you hit me back. That'll only improve my odds."

He shakes his head. "You have to take it that one step too far, don't you?"

"Always." I won't do it. I won't. I will not. "Sorry." Goddammit.

"Forget it," he mutters, waving a hand. "I won't tell on you."

"That's not why I said it." *Goddammit.* "Look, just give Becky another chance—"

"Only if you ease off on Jake Gardner."

"Ease off? I've only talked to him, like, three times."

"Yeah, and every one of those times you've been a bitch—"

"What is this? Have you taken a *shine* to the boy?"

He rolls his eyes. "Yeah, Parker. That's exactly it."

"Well, why didn't you say so? I'll lighten up on him then."

"Really?"

"No. God, do you know who you're talking to?"

"Unfortunately," Chris says. The bell explodes in my head or rings, whatever. I wince and rub my temples. "And consider this a favor. If you come to school hungover again, I'll go straight to Grey."

"*Thanks,* Chris."

"You're *welcome,* Parker."

Becky makes a mad dash into the room a minute after the Pledge of Allegiance starts over the PA and I wonder if she's avoiding Chris, like if their date went that bad. After we recite the Apostles' Creed, I move back to where she's sitting despite Chris's best efforts to convince me not to.

"How'd the date go?" I ask.

She smiles. "Okay. Chris is a great guy."

It's enough to make a girl depressed. When Chris says Becky's a *great girl* it means she's boring, but when Becky says Chris is a *great guy* it means she's probably started a scrapbook of the time they've spent together.

"Details, details," I sing. "Where did you go and what did you do and do you have a Tylenol on you? I've got a killer headache."

She unzips her pencil case and retrieves a Baggie of white pills and I can't help but laugh at how suspect it looks. I help myself to two and swallow them dry.

"We went for a ride around and we stopped at that diner out on Route Seven. It was mostly just talking, you know. He talked about you a lot. Like, the whole night was mostly about Parker, actually. It was lovely."

I pretend she didn't say it.

"Did you make plans for a second date?"

"No," she says. "I don't think there'll be one."

"What? Come on! You said he's a great guy!"

"I also said he talked about you for the whole date."

She says it with a voice that totally hates me, even though I can't be held responsible for Chris being such a fuck. We stare at each other. It's way easier to not be Becky's friend than it is to not be Chris's girlfriend.

"He liked the sweater, though," she adds. "A lot."

My head buzzes through history while I wait for the Tylenol to kick in. By the time art rolls around I feel less hungover and more charitable. We're working with paint today and I pick the easel next to Jake's. It thrills him.

"What do *you* want?"

"I want to apologize if you're offended by the way I am," I tell him. "But that's the way I am with everyone. I was just trying to make you feel welcome."

"That's the crappiest apology I've ever heard."

"Well, that's because I'm not really sorry."

He rolls his eyes. "Right."

We get to painting. I wish I could have art forever. Senior art, anyway. Norton's a hard-ass, but a lazy one. At our age, he figures, we've learned everything about art that can be learned in high school, and now we spend the entire period trying to create things that he might not have seen in the last twenty-five years. Every forty minutes is another opportunity to surprise him. The bigger the surprise, the better the mark.

"So, where do you come from and how come you moved here?"

Jake reaches for the red paint. "West Coast. My dad wanted a new scene."

"He couldn't have waited until the end of the year?"

Jake snorts. "Nope."

"And how are you finding St. Peter's? Do you like it here so far?"

He gives me a look. "Generally."

What can I say? I stare at the paper in front of me and try to figure out what to create. I glance across the room, at Chris's easel. Sure enough, he's painting a tree. I grin, reach for the black and get to work on a stick person.

A stick person with its head on fire.

"So, what's your deal?"

It takes a minute before I realize Jake's talking to me. There's something very enthralling about painting a stick person with its head aflame.

You just forget the rest of the world.

"What do you mean?"

"I heard you used to be captain of the cheerleading squad."

"Now where did you hear a crazy thing like that?"

"Chris mentioned it."

"Then it must be true."

"He said you used to be popular."

"Mentioned that, too, did he?"

"I asked, but if you were head cheerleader, I guess I didn't need to. I was surprised. Not many people give up those kinds of perks."

"Hmm."

I think I'll turn this stick person into Chris. All I have to do is put an orange jersey with the number 22 on it and he'll know it's him.

"So, what's your deal?" Jake asks again.

"Jake, I barely know you."

I spend lunch in the gym again, watching the boys scrimmage and the girls eating carrot sticks before they get ready to cheer. This kind of routine could get monotonous fast, and not in a good way.

I stretch out on the bleachers, shoving aside the lunch Mom packed for me. My headache is gone, but I don't think I can handle food. I shouldn't have finished off the bottle of vodka in my room last night. It was left over from before, hidden in the back of my closet, and I drank until I fell asleep. That's the only reason to do it now and I don't do it very often, contrary to what everyone else thinks. Back then, I drank to be caught. It was the start of my great campaign to distance myself from everyone. I even had a checklist and everything. First item: indulge in alienating, self-destructive behavior.

It worked beautifully at the start, but I hadn't counted on my family and former friends conspiring against me. The problem with alienating, self-destructive behavior is people get it into their heads it's a cry for help. It wasn't. It was just a really poorly executed plan to get everyone off my back. So now I'm halfway between where I started (not alone) and where I want to end up (alone) and I just have to roll with it if I want to graduate or else I'll never be alone. It's stupid. And not just because of the homework thing. Oh shit.

Lerner's essay.

Shit.

I tear out of the gym with such zeal the boys stop playing and the girls stop cheering to watch me go. I rip my English binder and pencil case from my locker and find the page Becky gave me with the assignment on it.

Write a thousand-word essay comparing how you relate to "The Yellow Wallpaper" as a senior to how you related to the story as a freshman.

My headache flares up. I press my palms against my eyes and try to wish, wish, wish myself out of this situation.

A thousand words?

I sit down, my back against my locker, and glare at the opposite wall, right into the eyes of Jessica Wellington. Jessie. Her photograph, anyway. I forgot. Four years, two suicides, one death, one rape, two pregnancies (one abortion), three overdoses and one missing person. Jessica Wellington. Since late junior year. Just up and ran away.

I'd give anything to be her right now.

So it's one missed essay. What's the worst they could do? Maybe I'll cry in front of Lerner. He *hates* that. He grants extensions at the drop of a hat if girly tears are involved. It's what he's famous for.

"Parker?"

Chris. He sits beside me, arm close enough to touch mine. I resist the urge to flee. I can't stand being around him in class, but it's easier than being around him alone.

"Didn't you get enough of me in homeroom?" I ask.

"Are you okay? Your exit from the gym was . . . startling."

"I forgot to do an essay for Lerner over the weekend, which wouldn't be that big of a deal if it wasn't a point against me graduating with the rest of you at the end of the year."

"Bet you wish you hadn't gotten drunk on Sunday now."

I bat my eyelashes at him. "Chris, I believe you don't feel sorry for me."

"I think you do it to yourself."

"Of course I do." I should at least be trying for a thousand words, but I don't. I just sit there while he stares at me. "What?"

"You were right."

"I'm right about lots of things. Be more specific."

"Becky's not you and that's why I don't want to date her again."

I laugh.

"Many girls aren't me. You'd better get used to it."

"Can't."

"Why? I did awful things to you and I'd do them all over again."

He winces. "I don't think you meant them."

"I meant them."

"You know, that '94 issue of *Cosmopolitan* didn't have anything in it about G-spots," he says. "But I should've figured you were lying."

"Yeah, you should've."

"But Becky *does* know where it is." My mouth drops open. I try to recover, but it's too late; Chris saw it. I don't know why I expected Becky to tell me something like that. He smiles. "Doesn't bother you, does it?"

"No." I swallow. "Okay, so *why* exactly can't you go out

on a second date? If it doesn't bother you that she's not me when you fuck her, I don't see why you can't—"

He holds up his hand. "We didn't fuck."

"Oh, I see. Congratulations."

"Where do you think she is?"

"What are you talking about?"

He nods at the poster of Jessica. "Where do you think she is?"

"Dead," I say. "Either that or working as a prostitute. But probably dead."

"Nice. I can't believe you just said that." He blows a strand of hair out of his eyes. "You didn't used to be this cold."

"You know, if I do my homework and I don't come to school hungover anymore, it's still going to be like this. It's not a phase, Chris. This is who I am."

"Do you ever hear yourself?" he asks. "You're so full of shit."

"No, I'm *not* anymore. That's the point."

He grabs my arm and leans forward, unbearably close. His lips graze my neck and get close to my mouth. I shiver.

"Fuck off, Chris."

He lets me go and stands.

"Good luck with your essay."

He heads back in the direction of the gym. I reopen my binder and poise my pen above the blue lines. I should at least try.

Write a thousand-word essay comparing how you relate to "The Yellow Wallpaper" as a senior to how you related to the story as a freshman.

I didn't even reread the stupid story and the only memory I have of it isn't entirely accurate, if I'm to believe Becky, which in this case I do. Still, I'm a fantastic liar in all other aspects of my life, so writing a thousand-word lie should be easy.

I can do it. I can do this.

As a freshman, I found "The Yellow Wallpaper" to be—

Fuck it, I'll just cry.

four

I'm a fantastic crier. Everyone is on suicide watch.

Plus: I don't have to do the essay.

Minus: it landed me in Grey's office and she called my parents.

Plus: we're getting a dog this Saturday!

On Tuesday, Norton surprises everyone by giving us an honest-to-God project that will take up a huge chunk of our time and account for a huge chunk of our grade and I don't like him so much anymore.

"Two sides of the same landscape," he announces, standing before us like Patton. "That's what this project is about. You'll pair up—"

Norton's momentarily interrupted by the sound of screeching chairs as best friends skirt close, claiming one another. You don't want to wind up with someone like me for a partner. He frowns.

"On second thought, *I'll* put you into pairs—" Everyone groans. "Quiet."

Chris glances at me. Bet he was going to ask.

"Two sides of the same landscape," Norton repeats in his gravelly voice. "Here's what you're going to do: You're going to arrange a time to meet with your partner to scout the local landscape and take a picture of it. You'll bring that picture to class. Are you all with me so far?"

I'm bored already.

"You will, as partners, proceed to paint the left and right side of the landscape, respectively, using the photo as a reference for the *base*. I want you to reimagine the landscape itself. The colors, the season—turn a paradise into wasteland! There is one caveat: you and your partner must reimagine each side of your landscape independently and figure out a way to bring it together to form a whole. I want unity and disparity here, people! Surely with everything I've taught you, you can manage *that*."

I've never seen Norton so excited. He's dancing on the balls of his feet and I imagine him lying awake in bed late last night, the idea coming to him like a flash of lightning. He bolts upright and shouts, *Eureka! A new way to torture my second-period senior class!* Or something.

Chris raises his hand.

"I don't get it, sir."

Norton surveys the room. "Does everyone else here get it?"

No one says anything.

"Looks like it's just you, Ellory, but at least you'll be partnered with someone who does and has the time to explain it to you slowly and repeatedly until you understand."

I can't help it; I laugh. Chris glares at me and Norton starts pairing us up. Every set of names called is met with either groans of derision or happy little shrieks of joy from all sides of the room. I hold my breath, expecting Chris because it would just be my life to have to fend his lips off my neck while we scout the area and take pictures, but it's not Chris; it's Jake.

Which seems so much more obvious in hindsight.

"Fadley and Gardner."

"Shit," Jake mutters. I waggle my eyebrows at him.

He rests his head on the table all *kill me now*.

After the bell rings, he approaches me very, very cautiously. It makes me feel very, very intimidating. I like that.

"Let's make this as painless as possible," he says. "When do you want to start scouting out locations? Tomorrow?"

"Whoa, slow down. Tomorrow's too soon."

"It's a huge project," he says. "It's probably not soon enough."

I pull out my ponytail and retie it, thinking. It would've been easier if he'd volunteered to take the pictures himself, and from what he already knows about me I don't know why he didn't. A couple minutes pass.

Jake clears his throat. "Oh, sure, feel free to take your time. It's not like I want to eat lunch or hang in the gym or anything."

So I let a couple more minutes pass.

"How about Friday after school?" I finally suggest. "I have a meeting at the guidance office last period. You can meet me there when class lets out. Bring a note so you can come on my bus—"

"I already go on your bus. Our bus, actually."

I blink. "You do not."

"Yeah, I do," Jake says in a *duh* voice. "Bus four-twenty-six is my bus, too. I've been on it every day since I started here and I've seen you on it. You sit at the front."

"This is fascinating. I never even noticed you."

I try to recall the seating arrangement, but I can't. The bus is worse than school. At least at school there are a couple of places I can hide, but there's nowhere on the bus. I usually sit at the front, close my eyes and open them at my stop.

"Do you sit at the back?"

"Near the middle," he says. "Anyway, Friday's fine. See you then."

Nothing happens Wednesday and almost nothing happens Thursday until I accidentally overhear Becky and Chris schedule their second date for Saturday. I make a mental note to find out the time they're taking off so I can sneak into his backyard again.

"You said you felt overwhelmed on Monday," Grey says. "Let's talk about that."

"What else do you want me to say? I was overwhelmed."

"Actually, I was thinking 'hysterical' would be a more apt description. . . ."

The thing about crying in Lerner's was once I started, I couldn't stop. I didn't even mean it or really feel it, but I couldn't stop. I could waste time analyzing that, but I won't. It got me out of the essay and it's getting me a dog. That's all that matters.

"The moment got away from me, I guess," I say.

But Grey wants more than that, like last time, and even though I'm kind of bored, like last time, I don't want to overextend myself. I need that energy to take pictures with Jake after the bell.

Fridays are turning out to be a major pain in the ass.

I shrug. "Maybe it was because it felt too much like . . . before?"

"You mentioned that last Friday, things feeling like before," Grey says. She opens her Parker notebook. "It seemed to be a good thing then. What's changed?"

I stare at the inspirational poster tacked to the wall behind her head. Something about not giving up. Lame.

"I had a lot of responsibilities," I say. "I was thinking about it. I was captain of the cheerleading squad, I was a straight A-plus student and, let's be honest, I was popular. All of that takes *a lot* of work. I did some stupid things and lost it all, but that also meant I got rid of all those responsibilities and you know what? I liked life a lot better. Before, I was suffocating. So, lately, I've been trying for the homework thing, because I want to graduate, but that essay . . . every time I sat down to write it, I just *couldn't* because—"

"You felt suffocated," Grey finishes.

She's so smart. I mean, *I'm* so smart. She's so predictable.

"Yeah."

"Well, I sympathize, Parker, but we can't make many more allowances for you. As it stands, we've—"

"I wasn't asking," I say, laughing a little. "I mean, it's not like I cried in Lerner's on *purpose.*"

Shit. It comes out of my mouth wrong, like I *did* cry on purpose, which I did, but Grey's obviously not supposed to know that. And of course she catches it.

Her face darkens.

"Ms. *Grey!*" I bring my hand to my mouth and try to sound scandalized, to diffuse the situation. "You don't think I did it on purpose, do you?"

But *that* comes out of my mouth wrong, too.

"You just don't learn, do you, Parker?" She closes her notebook and glares at me. "You run everyone around in circles—"

"I run everyone around in circles?"

"You do."

"I do?"

"Stop that." She takes off her glasses and rubs her eyes. "You want everyone to think your problem is what happened over the summer—"

"No, that's what everyone *wants* to think—"

"But it *is* your problem!" She puts her glasses back on. "You manipulate. You make it your excuse and that's exactly how you push it away."

The party starts at eight, but I show up early so Chris and I can have sex. Another year at St. Peter's is almost behind us and we've already slept together eight times. This will be the ninth and there's going to be a lot more sex in our future.

We go to his bedroom. The speakers are mounted against his window and he turns on some sweet-sounding music really low and he kisses me and I kiss him back and then, I don't know, I kind of seize up.

"What's wrong?"

"That doesn't even make any sense," I tell Grey.

It's the last thing I tell her. We sit in silence until the bell rings. I feel like I should be furious with her, and I might be, but more than that, I'm annoyed. I have to remind myself she wasn't there and she doesn't know a damn thing so I can't really blame her for making half-assed assertions once a week. I just wish she wouldn't.

When I get out, Jake's waiting for me at the door.

We head outside.

I can't believe he goes on my stupid bus and I didn't even notice.

"You can sit where you normally sit," I tell him.

"Don't worry; I was going to," he replies. "So do you have any idea—"

"Yeah, I have an idea: please stop talking."

We climb on the bus. I take my usual seat at the front and he heads for the middle. I rest my head against the window and close my eyes. I don't mean to, but I fall asleep, and fifteen minutes later Jake's shaking my shoulder and looking pretty irritated. All through art he pestered me, "Where are we going? What are we taking pictures of. . . ."

"I *think* this is your stop," he says sarcastically.

I rub my eyes. "Yeah."

We inch up the aisle and step onto the street. I can see my house from here, but I don't want to go through the hassle of introducing Jake to my parents because they'd interpret it all wrong and it'd give them false hope and, like I said before, I don't do that.

"We'll go this way." I point in the opposite direction. "If we go down this street, turn left and walk through the park there's this kind of wooded area. Beyond that, there's a ravine. We could probably get some really good pictures there."

"We're not going to your house first?"

"I don't want you to know where I live."

He laughs. "Like I give a damn. But sure, let's go to the ravine."

We walk. I don't know if I should be nice to him or if this technically makes him my guest because we're near where I live and he has no idea where we are.

"So you and Chris really hit it off, huh?"

I keep my voice light and conversational, but Jake still seems to weigh every word like he's trying to figure out which one of them is poisoned.

"He's cool," he says after a while. "I mean, he didn't treat me like a new kid, you know? We hang."

"He and Becky are going out—you know Becky, right? Becky Halprin? She's captain of the cheerleading squad. Anyway, they had a date last Friday and they're having another one this weekend, I think."

"Yeah, Saturday," Jake says. "It's not really a date, though. A couple of us are going to go shoot some pool at Finn's, wherever that is."

"Finn Walters?"

"Yeah, you know him?"

"Yeah. He's on the chess team. He's, like, this superintellectual and yet still cool." It could be all the blow he deals in the boys' washrooms. "So it's a night thing, right? When are you going? Around eight?"

"Chris says he'll pick me up at—" He stops. "Why? Are you fishing for an invite or something? Because you're not going to get one from me."

"I've got better things to do with a Saturday night, but thanks."

"Like what?"

"Like not hanging out with you?"

"Walked right into that one, didn't I?"

"Yeah, you did."

We laugh. And then we realize we're laughing together and then we stop and then it gets awkward. I don't do awkward well, at least mutual awkwardness, so I snap my fingers to make the feeling go away.

And then I can't stop.

Even after Jake points it out.

"That's really annoying," he says.

So I kick it up a notch just to bug him and I keep it up until my fingers start to hurt.

We trek through the park and enter the woods beyond it. They're not like the woods by Chris's house. They're a little denser, a little easier to get lost in, but I'm not worried. I like them. Nothing bad happened here and it makes the air less polluted, somehow. It doesn't make me want to throw up.

"It's really great out here," I say without thinking. "There's nothing—"

I shut my mouth.

"What?" Jake asks.

"Nothing. We'll get good pictures out here, that's all."

He reaches into his book bag and pulls out his phone.

"But not here—it's a little farther in. Give me that." I hold out my hand and he steps back, clutching the phone to his chest. "Oh, come on, Jake. I'm not going to steal or break it. I may not respect people, but I do respect their property."

He groans and hands it to me.

"I must be crazy."

"You're right; you are."

I take it and run and the look on his face is *so great*.

"Parker!"

He has no choice but to chase after me, and I have a hell of a lead. I can hear my pulse pounding in my ears and the air is cold and sharp in my lungs and I like that. I get to the ravine ages before him, scale the nearest tree—which is also the biggest and the oldest—and wriggle my way along the thickest branch out.

The one that hovers directly above the thirty-foot drop.

When Jake finally catches up to me, I'm dangling from a pretty precarious angle, nearly upside down, and it probably looks terrifying from where he's standing.

But it will be so worth this shot.

"Are you trying to kill yourself?" he yells, panting.

I keep my leg muscles tight around the branch so I don't, you know, die.

"If I was trying to kill myself, I'd make sure you weren't here."

"Parker, get down from there. You're making me nervous—"

"Coward."

"Fuck off."

A little more . . .

The branch makes a few disconcerting creaking noises, but I'm going to pretend it's not giving out under my weight. I open the camera app, the view making me slightly dizzy, and get a good focus on the ravine. The edges of either side of it creep up the corners of the frame.

Jake's either holding his breath or wetting himself.

Got it.

I right myself, snake backward and hold his phone out.

"Catch!"

"Parker, no—"

I let it go. It seems to fall in slow motion. Jake catches it like I knew he would and he starts swearing at me like I knew he would. When he's finished, he checks out the shot.

"Decent," he mutters. "But you're lucky I caught my phone."

The branch I'm on protests a little more. I stand very, very carefully and maneuver my way to a branch on the opposite side. It's tricky.

"You're good at that," Jake says, as I settle on my new branch.

"I've lived in trees my whole life."

"Do you have some kind of retort for everything?"

"I'm the straightest talker you've ever met."

"Oh, really? I think most of what comes out of your mouth is—"

And that's when the goddamn branch gives out.

five

The fall takes no time and forever.

I land on my feet for a split second and then my legs crumple and I'm flat on my back and I don't know whether to laugh or cry or swear because I can't believe the *other* branch broke, so I just lay there not moving instead.

"Jesus—Parker?" Dead leaves crunch under Jake's feet as he hurries over. I should say something. He kneels down. "Parker? Are you okay?"

"I can't feel my legs."

He turns white. "Are you serious?"

"No."

"Not funny," he snaps. "You're okay?"

"I'm fine."

I prop myself up on my elbow and ignore the insistent, toothachelike pain going on in my right ankle. Jake doesn't need to know about that.

"Nice catch," I say.

He laughs and stands, brushing the dirt from his knees.

"Like I was gonna catch *you*. Come on, let's get out of here; it's getting dark."

I extend my hands. Jake looks surprised, but he grabs me by the wrists and hoists me up. I stumble into him. Busted. He gives me a look.

"You hurt yourself, didn't you?"

"Nothing's broken."

"But you hurt yourself, didn't you?"

"I've had worse injuries on the cheerleading squad."

"Parker," Jake says impatiently. "What hurts?"

"Ankle."

"There, that wasn't so hard, was it?" He pauses and looks awkward. "Uh . . . do you need to lean on me or—"

"*No,*" I say emphatically. "I'm good for limping, thanks."

"I have this crazy feeling you'd say that even if you weren't."

We make our way back through the woods. I take a sharp breath in for every step forward, but I don't think it's anything serious. I'll get the compress out when I get home and I'll be good for Monday or I could run up and down the stairs until it's so inflamed I couldn't possibly make it to school.

But I'll give Jake credit. He slows his pace to accommodate my stupid injury and he doesn't go tearing off into the woods like I might've done to him.

I kind of wish he would, though, as he feels the need to pass the time by talking.

"So what'd you do that you have to see Ms. Grey once a week?"

"Run-of-the-mill-delinquent stuff," I say. "It's none of your business."

"Okay."

Limp, limp, limp.

"I got drunk at school. A lot. Earlier this year."

I only admit it because it's something he probably already knows. People talk. I can't be the first person he's asked about me.

He shoves his hands in his pockets. "Do you have, like . . . a problem?"

"Yeah, and that was my solution." He looks all uncomfortable and I laugh. "Lighten up. If I say I don't, you wouldn't believe that, right? Anyone who says they don't have a drinking problem usually does."

"Do they?" he asks. I take a hard step on my ankle and gasp. He pauses, but I wave him off before he can ask if I'm okay. We keep moving and he starts talking again. God, I wish he'd shut up. "So why did you drink?"

"I—" Limp, limp, limp. "What does Chris tell you about me?"

"He said the pressures of being popular made your brain snap."

"Seriously?"

"Yeah."

I'm so touched; he lied for me. Might as well go along with it.

"It was something like that, yeah."

"I'm sorry it was so hard for you," Jake says. He *means* it. And then he gets quiet, but now *I* want to talk.

"Do you feel you know me a little better now?" I ask.

He gives me an appraising look.

"You're not that bad."

"It's the sprained ankle. It ups my likability because I can't kick your ass with a broken foot. You probably have a thing for girls when they're vulnerable because they make you feel so big and strong—"

"I take it back; you *are* that bad. You're—" He shakes his head. "Never mind; just shut up."

"You totally softened after I fell out of the tree. I'm just saying."

"Yeah, well, I think any decent human being would."

He picks up the pace. My ankle gives me no choice but to fall behind.

"*I* wouldn't," I say to his back.

We split up at the corner to my house after I give him directions to Chris's and it's tense and awkward and unhappy, but that's the way I like it. Jake should know—well, everyone should know—there's no such thing as a decent human being. It's just an illusion.

And when it's gone, it's really gone.

six

"WIN OR LOSE!
"IT'S ALL THE SAME!
"WE DO OUR BEST!
"WE'VE GOT GAME! . . ."

"Stop!" I shout. I don't even want to hear the rest of it.

The girls stare at me, frozen in a ludicrous pose, arms up and out. They remind me of Barbie dolls wearing orange and yellow. This is a new cheer. Becky tabled it. I didn't want to do it, but she begged for months. "You have to let us try it, Parker! The girls will be great!"

But they're not great. They suck and the cheer sucks.

"No," I tell them. "Absolutely not. It's a cheer about being okay with losing—how can you think that's appropriate on any level, Becky? Do you want us to look like fools when we play against St. Mary's?"

"*It's not about being okay with losing,*" Becky snorts. "*It's about good sportsmanship!*"

I ignore her. "*Line up! We'll do the Victory chant for now and I'll figure out something else later, but forget this 'do our best' piece of shit. We're not doing it. And you were all terrible.*"

Becky's mouth drops open.

"*I'm sure she doesn't totally mean it like that, guys,*" *Jessie says, staring at me.*

Mom bursts into my room and opens the blinds. I pull the blankets over my head and groan. There's something about the early morning rays of sunshine beating down on my face that makes me want to puke.

"Today's a big day!" she announces. "How does your foot feel?"

"I don't know; I haven't stepped on it yet. Oh my *God*, Mom, would you close the blinds—"

"You should be excited! Today's the day we're bringing Bailey home!"

Bailey. The dog. We passed the interview process, filled out the adoption forms, and I chose the dog next in line to be put down, even though he's not a puppy, because I'm thoughtful like that. Bailey's a ten-year-old harrier with a happy disposition and I think he'll make a great daughter, for a dog.

Mom leaves. I swing my legs over the bed, touch my foot to the floor and stand. It feels better, but I doubt I'll be walking Bailey this week. Falling out of a tree was good for something; Mom or Dad can bond with the dog during the first few integral days and then they can forget he was ever supposed to be for me.

"Oh, Bailey, look, Bailey! Say hello to your new mommy and daddy and sister! Oh, that's a good boy!"

The shelter volunteer is this woman who slobbers nearly

as much as, if not more than, the many dogs surrounding us. Most of them are barking like crazy and there's something about the sound that goes straight to my stomach. The shelter is too small for the number of animals here and it's hot. I snap my fingers to make the feeling go away and glance at Bailey, who stares at me with these big golden-brown eyes. For a second, it's weird. I feel like I'm doing something good, but not just for me.

"Now, Bailey, you be *good,* you hear me?" The woman kneels and gives Bailey such a long hug I think he'll suffocate and die. "We'll miss you. . . ."

Oh my God, I think she's crying.

Sure enough, when she stands, her eyes are bright and her cheeks are damp. Weak, especially considering they were gearing Bailey up to die in a couple of days anyway. The woman passes the leash to Dad, stifles another sob and wishes us well. Bailey's strangely calm about the whole thing. Even the car ride home. Maybe he'll be such a good dog we won't even know we have him.

When we get home, he explores each room at his leisure, sniffing at anything and everything, every nook and cranny. He does it with a practiced disinterest and I wonder what his deal is. His last owner was abusive.

Bailey edges up to the door of my room.

"Bailey." He turns and looks at me. "No."

I block his path and close the door so he can't get in. And then I say it again:

"No. That's *my* room. You're not allowed in there."

He just looks at me and wags his tail. I hold my hand out and he sniffs it.

"So what did you do that no one wanted you, huh?"

I crouch down and scratch him under the chin, behind the ears. I think he likes it; I don't know. We've never had a pet before.

"One of you should take him for a walk soon," I call down the hall to my parents. "I would, but I can't on this foot."

Mom and Dad decide to make it a family outing and walk him together.

It's already working.

I have to sneak out later that night. I lock my bedroom door and crawl out the window. The trip to Chris's takes longer with a sore ankle and sneaking around his house becomes less graceful, but I wind up in the woods all the same, on my hands and knees, digging while the ghost music thrums in the background. I don't throw up this time, but there's a feeling in the pit of my gut that tells me I could.

After a while, I stop looking. There's nothing here. I know that.

I *know* that.

But there was something here.

I rub my wrist and let my fingers drift over the bracelet. This was here. Delicate, thin and gold. It should've been impossible for me to find, but I found it. Weeks and weeks after the fact. I did a terrible thing and I get to wear it on my wrist. And I guess I sort of hope there will be more of these kinds of things here, waiting for me to find them even though I know, logically, there won't be. Still, I have to come out and look because the feeling that there *might* be won't go away until I do.

And then it goes away.

Until it comes again.

Monday, my foot feels fine. I stave off zoning out on the bus just so I can see Jake get on. Our eyes meet when he climbs aboard. He shrugs his book bag over his shoulder and it kind of seems like he's going to say something, but he doesn't. He finds his spot in the middle.

"Got a dog, huh?"

I pause and look down at Chris. He looks up at me. His math homework is open on his desk, half-done. He pulls out the chair beside him.

"I saw your parents walking it. Sit."

I raise an eyebrow. *"Sit?"*

"Would you please sit down?"

I toss my books on the desk and do as I'm told.

"I'm so behind in math," I say, staring at his book. "A full unit behind, almost two. I haven't even bothered trying to catch up. Maybe I'll just drop out. It'd save me the trouble of working this hard to graduate."

"That's always one option," Chris says. "Heard you fell out of a tree last Friday."

"Heard you were at Finn's. High times?"

"Not all visits to Finn's end in drug use. There were a lot of us there. Just shot the shit, introduced Jake to some people. Good party, I guess."

"You used to throw good parties."

"Didn't I, though." He looks away. "I could get used to Becky. I was thinking about it. Wouldn't be so bad. Just for senior year."

"Lucky Becky."

"Like I said, I'm thinking about it. It's ill-befitting someone of my popularity to go as long as I have single, which is your fault."

"You think you can make me feel guilty?"

"I'm trying."

Just like that, I'm tired of this conversation. I grab my books and stand even though it's not like I have somewhere else to go. The bell will ring in ten minutes.

But in ten minutes I could be far away.

"Sit," he says again. I sit and reach for his pencil. Twirl it between my fingers.

"You can't make me feel guilty," I tell him. "About any of it."

And now it's not just about Becky anymore.

He opens his mouth and closes it. Opens it. Closes it again.

"Or sorry," I add. "You can't make me sorry about any of it, either."

"Okay," Chris says, "but whether or not you're sorry or guilty doesn't change the fact that I forgive you anyway. And I don't blame you."

"Yes, you do."

"I don't."

"You do. You're just saying that because you want to—"

"I *don't* blame you, Parker. You weren't thinking clearly—"

"Why are we talking about this?"

I have no patience for this kind of bullshit. It's like now that I'm seeing Grey everyone's all, *Oh, she must have her head on straight, so I can move in again,* which is what I was afraid of, but no one gets to move in ever again because it's better for everyone this way. People are so stupid. They don't even know when you're helping them.

"You brought it up," he says, and then he smiles. "You know, we could work something out. You be my girlfriend again, I give you my math homework . . ."

"Right."

"Okay, skip the girlfriend thing and let's make it sexual favors."

I can't tell if he's serious or not.

"Do I look that cheap to you?" I ask.

When Becky enters the room, he moves to the back to sit beside her.

"WIN OR LOSE!

"IT'S ALL THE SAME!

"WE DO OUR BEST!

"WE'VE GOT GAME!"

I'm dreaming again. I pinch myself. Ouch. Not dreaming. It's lunchtime in the gym and Becky is actually leading the cheerleading squad in that stupid cheer.

"—Unity and disparity. I've been thinking about this a lot and I'm totally confused—"

"Did you hear that?'

Jake looks up from his spot beside me on the bleachers.

"What?"

"The cheer about losing. Did you hear it?"

"Uh, not really," he says, annoyed. "See, I was talking about our *art project*—"

"Shut up; they're doing it again. Listen. It's really awful."

The girls resume triangle formation, Becky at the point of it.

"One, two, three!"

The cheer starts up again. Jake and I watch, transfixed. The beat is painfully off, the dance steps contrived and awkward. Cardboard cutouts of cheerleaders operated by arthritic monkeys would move more fluidly.

They finish and Jake—bless his heart—says, "Yeah, that was pretty bad."

"You suck, Becky!" I shout.

The cheerleaders twitter. Becky places her hands on her hips and turns to me. I've heard around the halls there's nothing more terrifying than being glared at by St. Peter's High's cheerleading captain, but that was when *I* was the captain.

When Becky glares, it's just funny.

"There was a reason I wouldn't let us do that cheer, you know," I say.

She frowns.

"You're not captain anymore. You don't get a say in it."

"Yeah, and you might not be captain for much longer. They'll oust you from the squad if you perform that at the next game."

The girls twitter some more, but I can't tell if it's agreeable twittering. They should know from past experience I'm always right about stuff like this.

Becky orders them to take a break and storms up the bleachers to me.

"Uh-oh . . . ," Jake says under his breath.

"Fuck off, Parker," Becky says when she reaches me. "That's my squad out there. *My* squad. Not yours, *mine*. How *dare* you humiliate me in front of the girls—"

I burst out laughing.

"It's an awful cheer and you know it. You think you'll prove me wrong by performing it? You think I actually care? Because I don't—"

"Then why did you feel the need to mouth off while we were practicing it? You wouldn't have tolerated that from anyone, and if I remember correctly, you *didn't*—"

"Jessie would've vetoed that in a second if she was here, and she *did* the last time you tried to get us to do it. Remember?"

"Jessie's not here, you bitch."

She storms back down the bleachers.

"Becky, I lied!" I yell. She doesn't turn around. "I do care. The squad will look like total douche bags if they perform that cheer."

She returns to the girls. I rest my chin in my hands.

"Are you ready to talk about our project now?"

"No," I say.

"Okay, good," Jake says exasperatedly. "So basically, Norton is fucked. Unity and disparity is . . . ridiculous. But I was thinking we should do one side really, really, really dark and the other side really, really, really light—"

"But how do you connect that? It has to connect in the middle."

"Right. Damn it." He groans and stares longingly at the game of basketball Chris & Co. are having on the court.

"Let's make it subtle," I say. "Maybe one side can be spring and the middle can be summer and the other side can be fall. . . ."

Jake nods eagerly. "I like that!"

"Oh, really? I thought you wouldn't. We can't do that. That's what Mindy Andrews and Cory Hall are doing. I overheard them."

He rolls his eyes and checks out the cheerleaders.

"Do you miss it?" he asks.

"No."

It's not true. I kind of miss cheerleading sometimes. The squad. Just for something to do, to distract myself with. I know they don't miss me. I was a nightmare captain and they had to be perfect. But I was like that about everything. My grades, my relationship with Chris, my friends. Everything perfect.

The bell rings.

"You didn't get to play," I say.

Jake sighs. "Yeah."

"You should try out for the team."

"Can't. My knee's all fucked up. I hurt it during the most important game of the season at my old school. Little games at lunch are about all I can stand. I miss it a lot." He sounds wistful. "I love basketball."

Great. Just more useless information I won't be able to forget.

seven

By Wednesday, word around the halls is Chris and Becky are a couple. By Thursday, it's confirmed. They've got the Public Displays of Affection thing down pat and I have to hand it to them, they look pretty happy for two people who have absolutely nothing to be happy about. He's with her because he can't be with me and she's got to suffer every kiss knowing that, and boy, does she know that.

By Thursday night, Bailey knows how to fetch Dad's slippers.

"Look at this!" Dad says, after he calls Mom and me into the living room. He's stretched out in his recliner and Bailey's sprawled out on the floor at his feet. Dad snaps his fingers. "Bailey!"

Bailey raises his head.

"Fetch, Bailey; fetch me my slippers, boy!"

It's terribly exciting. Bailey rises slowly, totters out of the room and totters back in with Dad's slippers in his mouth. Mom squeals a little and claps her hands.

This dog is mad talented.

"Good dog!" she gushes, patting Bailey on the head. He looks pretty satisfied with himself, for a dog. He nestles back into his spot at Dad's feet and Mom rushes into the kitchen to get him a treat.

"Good job, Bailey," I say.

But I'm not talking about the slippers.

The party starts at eight, but I show up early so Chris and I can have sex. Another year at St. Peter's is almost behind us and we've already slept together eight times. This will be the ninth and there's going to be a lot more sex in our future.

We go to his bedroom. The speakers are mounted against his window and he turns on some sweet-sounding music really low and kisses me and I kiss him back and then, I don't know, I kind of seize up.

"What's wrong?" he asks. He's breathing heavy.

We separate and I wipe my mouth.

"What have you been eating?"

"What does it matter?"

"Were you eating something with garlic in it? I told you not to eat garlic before you kiss me anymore. It's gross."

He sighs. "What's wrong, Parker?"

"You know I hate garlic breath and you eat it anyway, that's what's wrong."

"That's not what I mean."

I untie my ponytail and retie it. I think every so often, Chris should have to work for sex by listening to me.

"Jessie thinks I'm coming down on the other girls too hard."

"We stopped making out for that?"

He leans in for another kiss and I push him away.

"Fuck off, Chris. I'm serious."

"You're always serious."

"You say that like it's a bad thing."

"It can be." He flops back on his bed. "You should loosen the fuck up every once in a while; the world wouldn't stop. No one would die."

He's such a bastard. I loosen up, sometimes. And even if I didn't, it's not like there's something wrong with being focused. Some people are focused.

That's what they do.

"She says I'm coming down on the girls too hard," I repeat.

"Is she right?" he asks. "I bet she's right."

"I may have let them know how much they suck lately." The memory of their total suckiness gets me pissed off about it all over again. "But I want us to be good, you know? Is that too much to ask? I work my ass off thinking up cheers and dance moves and if they can't get them right, what, I'm supposed to congratulate them for it?"

Chris stares.

"It's just cheerleading."

"Oh, really? And if I said that about one of your basketball games—"

"That's different." He sits up and wraps an arm around me. "I've seen you captain. You're anal. You're anal about everything, though."

"I like things a certain way."

"You're a perfectionist. You like them perfect. There's no margin for error or you go crazy."

"If I can do things right, I don't see why everyone else can't." I untie my ponytail again and do it back up. "She called me a Cheerleading Dictator in front *of the entire squad. We got into a screaming match in front of everyone—"*

"That's so cute," Chris says, laughing. I glare at him and he stops. "Look, you'll see her in a couple of hours when the party's in full swing. Get her after she's had a couple shots and she's mellow. You can make up, no biggie. You're best friends. That's what you're supposed to do."

He kisses my neck.

"God, you're tense," he murmurs. "Maybe you should quit the squad, take a break or something. You're, like, this close to the edge—"

"That's funny, Chris," I interrupt.

"I'm not kidding. Loosen the fuck up." He kisses me again and slides his hand up my shirt. "Forget it. We'll talk about it later—"

"No," I say. "We won't."

My hand is wet. I open my eyes, hold it out in front of me and stare. Wet. *Tap, tap, tap.* Rain against the window. It's raining out and my hand is wet.

I sit up in bed, groggy. Is there a leak?

A loud clap of thunder startles me and there's a whimper at the side of my bed. I turn on the light. Bailey. It's three in the morning and he's been cowering on the floor, licking my hand. The thunder sounds again and he cries.

"Bailey, you're not allowed in my room." I climb out of bed and grab him by the collar. "Come on. Out."

He resists. I give his collar a sharp tug and he whimpers, anticipating the next round of thunder, but he can anticipate it in Mom and Dad's room for all I care. I lead him down the hall. Their door is closed, of course.

I let go of his collar.

"Stay," I say firmly.

He stays. I head back to my room and crawl back into

bed. The storm picks up. Every so often I hear Bailey whimpering and pawing at Mom and Dad's door and pretty soon I accept the fact I'm never getting to sleep again, so I get out of bed and find Bailey curled up in a terrified ball at the end of the hall. I slip my finger under his collar and we head downstairs to the living room.

A flash of lightning reveals Dad's armchair. I let Bailey go, grab an afghan and wrap myself in it. The dog sits beside me, frightened out of his mind. I reach out and run my hand over his head. I might scratch him behind the ears if I'm feeling particularly inspired. The thunder goes again and again and he shakes and cries.

"It's fine, Bailey," I say. "Don't be such a wimp. It's only a storm."

I wake up to Mom and Dad hovering over me. Bailey's asleep at my feet and—

Mom's holding the camera.

"You didn't," I say.

"That's one for the photo albums!" Dad winks at me. "You'd better hurry, Parker. You'll be late for school."

I hate my parents.

Chris and Becky enter homeroom joined at the hip and I make a gagging noise when they sit behind me, just because I can. Becky's still sore at me about cheerleading practice, so she calls me a bitch and excuses herself for the washrooms to confer about it with whatever minion she's got stationed there.

I turn to Chris as soon as she's gone.

"I've been thinking about the offer you made," I say. "About math."

He straightens. "Yeah?"

"I'm game if you are."

He looks around the room to make sure no one's overheard.

"Becky can't ever know," he says, an odd gravity to his voice.

"We'll see."

"Parker."

"Becky can't ever know." I hold up my hand. Scout's Honor. "Got it."

He frowns. "Meet me in the guys' change room at lunch."

"That soon, huh?"

"Just in case you change your mind."

Becky comes back five minutes later and Chris wraps his arms around her and they start sucking face. I know he's trying to make a statement, but I have no idea what that statement is. Bradley breaks them up when the Pledge of Allegiance starts, and we all stand, hands to hearts, hands to hearts—hands always to our hearts.

"If I tell you something about me, will you tell me something about you?"

Jake and I are sitting close, trying to sketch out the landscape in pencil before we start working with paint. Norton advises us to plan everything down to the most painstakingly minute details. It should be days turning into *weeks* before we get to the actual painting, he says. I think he doesn't want us to finish anytime soon, lest he be forced to think up new ways to occupy a class full of eighteen-year-olds. Either that or this is one of his cruel tricks where he waits until we're good and relaxed and tells us, whoops, his mistake, the project is actually due tomorrow and still counts for half our grades. That's the kind of teacher Norton is.

"No."

I've been tracing the same rocks for the last thirty minutes.

"Come on," Jake says. "I'm going to make you tolerate me if it kills me. Or you. Preferably you. But we should get to know each other on some level or else it will be impossible to work on this together."

"I don't know; it's working okay so far. And besides, what about you could I possibly want to know?"

"Try me. I will hold nothing back."

I decide to shock him into silence.

"Which do you prefer: top or bottom?"

His mouth drops open a little and I go back to my rocks. Mission accomplished.

"Up," he says unexpectedly. "Against the wall."

I laugh, my pencil hovering above the paper. "Right."

"Top."

I glance at him. "Really?"

"With my last girlfriend," he says. "More often than not."

"Sure. She still in the picture, this last girlfriend?"

"Dumped me when I told her I was moving."

"Ouch."

"Eh." Jake shrugs and works on the base of a tree stump. "We were together too long. How long were you and Chris together?"

"Why would I tell you that?"

"Because we agreed—"

"No, we didn't."

His eyebrows come together as he replays the conversation in his head and realizes I'm right, but I decide to go ahead and share because what I've chosen to share might make him realize I'm not a person worth getting to know. Get him off my back.

"Actually, Chris and I were together since the ninth grade.

We broke up after I stole about three hundred dollars from his savings account. Let that be a lesson to you, Jake: never give your high school sweetheart your PIN number, no matter how many times you've had sex or been Winter Ball King and Queen."

And that's not even the worst thing I've done. Jake studies me.

"Wow," he finally says. "Why'd you do that?"

"Gambling addiction," I say without missing a beat. "I spent all my money and some of his betting on horses and racked up a little debt. After a while Chris goes, 'Look, Parker, I'm not giving you any more money!' So I stole it from him."

"Actually, she ran away from home."

I plaster a bright smile on my face before turning around.

"Chris!" I say, all exaggerated cheer when I do. "And just how long have you been standing there?"

"Obviously long enough!" he says with a similarly exaggeratedly cheerful voice. He pushes past me, for Jake. "Anyway, Jake, I'm not going to be in the gym at lunch, so take center. Tell the guys I said you could. Aaron will want it, but I want to make Aaron cry like a little bitch for being such an asshole last Thursday."

Jake nods. "Center. Got it. Where will you be?"

"Nowhere special."

"Nowhere special" is a pretty apt description of the boys' changing room. It's rows of orange-painted lockers and square windows that filter weak rays of real light into the room—real light that's promptly swallowed by the fluorescent lights overhead.

And it smells bad.

Chris is sitting on the bench closest to the door when I sneak in. There's a binder resting beside him—math homework. At least it better be.

"What if someone comes in?" My voice echoes around the room.

Chris stands, drags the bench to the tiny alcove where the door is and wedges it in such a way that no one should be able to get in. There was definitely a time when he wouldn't have cared if anyone caught us in here—and we'd been caught a few times—but now he's with Becky and those days are dead.

"So." I clear my throat. "How many pages of math will this be worth?"

He nods to the bench. I sit. He sits beside me.

This is the skankiest thing I've ever done.

I try to ignore how it starts with his hands carefully coming up past my cheeks and around my neck until his fingers are in my hair. He doesn't kiss me then, but he brings his face close, forehead against mine, and breathes me in because he wants me to feel guilty, I think. I think maybe it's working.

I haven't thought about the money in a long time.

His lips get excruciatingly close to mine and he pauses.

"Do you even miss me?"

"No," I say.

He finally kisses me, presses his lips lightly against mine. I know what he's doing. He's teasing me and I won't have it. I make him *really* kiss me, full on the mouth, and force his lips apart with my own.

And then he stops.

"What about everything you felt about me? Where does that go?" He leans in again and stops before anything can happen. "I would've stuck it out. You wouldn't let me help you."

"I didn't need your help."

"Yes, you did. You do. Everyone got through it together but you. You're so perfect, you just couldn't handle it—"

"You're as bad as Jake," I say. "You talk too much. Shut up and forget it because it's not worth your homework for me to sit here and listen to you nitpick the past."

That kills it. After a second, he presses his binder into my hands.

"Take it," he says, before I can ask. "Have it back to me by tomorrow morning."

"Oh, come on. Afraid you won't respect yourself afterward?" I study him. His cheeks are pink. "I'm not going to tell Becky."

"I just wanted to kiss you again."

"Stop it."

"You could've said no," he says, standing. He pulls the bench out. "You know I'm not over you. You could've said no and done the homework yourself, but you didn't."

"You're right," I say. "You know what? You're absolutely right. Call it a momentary lapse of sanity."

He opens the door.

"Or maybe you just wanted to kiss me again, too."

I roll my eyes.

eight

Bailey's developed this weird attachment to me. He follows me from room to room, lays at my feet under the dinner table and stands guard in the living room for the two hours it takes me to copy Chris's math homework. My parents can't shut up about how *cute* it is, so three guesses for how I feel about it, and the first two don't count.

"Maybe you could take him for a walk, now that your foot is better."

Mom says it in a voice that tells me it's less of a suggestion and more of a command. I go along with it because I want out. I throw my coat on, attach Bailey to the leash—his tail wags back and forth excitedly—and escape.

"Hey, Parker!"

I've been walking a good forty minutes when I hear my name. Somehow I took a turn that landed me on Victoria Street, where the traffic is kind of heavy and I cross the paths of more people than I normally like to do. I cock my head to the side. Nothing. Maybe I didn't hear it after all. I keep walking.

"Parker!"

Damn. I turn in the direction of the voice and spot Jake emerging from the grocery store, a bag of groceries in hand. He jogs over.

"Didn't figure I'd see you before tomorrow," he says.

"That makes two of us."

"Who's this?"

Jake crouches down and gives Bailey a vigorous head petting. He scratches Bailey behind his ears, under his chin, the works.

"This is Bailey. Bailey, this is Jake Gardner."

"Hi, Bailey," Jake says, patting his nose. Bailey loves the attention. His eyes half close and his tongue hangs out, but his tongue always does that. I realize it's been thirty seconds and I haven't said anything mean to Jake.

Jake smiles at me. "I think Bailey likes me."

"Bailey doesn't have very discriminating taste," I warn him. "He adored his last owner and his last owner used to beat him, so it doesn't really say much about you."

Still got it.

Jake gives Bailey one last pat on the head and stands.

"So why did you run away from home?"

"How many minutes a day do you spend thinking about me?" I ask. "Like, do you have anything else to live for?"

"It's your own fault," he replies. "The less you want me to know about you, the more I want to find out. Especially if it bothers you."

"Nice. What gives you the right?"

"You kind of set the precedent when we met, didn't you?"

"Bailey, attack!"

I give his leash a sharp tug. He only stares at us happily. Jake laughs. "So cute."

"Yeah, well, I don't know about you, but I'm walking now."

"Wow, that's practically an invitation coming from you."

So we walk.

"Got any more ideas for our project?" he asks.

"I'm supposed to be thinking of ideas?" I ask back. "I wonder if Norton knows how dumb this assignment is. Do you think he does? Think he's just fucking with us?"

"I don't know, maybe. So why did you run away from home?"

"Okay, Jake?" I stop; he stops. "I'm going to tell you something and I want you to listen carefully and then every time you want to ask me a personal question, you can just refer back to this answer. Are you ready?"

He nods and his hair falls into his eyes. He brushes it away.

"I'm really fucked up," I tell him. "And I don't like people."

"Got it," he says. "But why?"

"It doesn't matter why. I don't give the people I *know* valuable insight into my psyche. You're the new kid. You have no chance."

"I'm going to try to have a conversation with you anyway. Are you ready?"

I think if I roll my eyes any more this year, they might get stuck in my head, so I refrain. But not rolling my eyes leaves me with an anxious feeling, so I hand Jake Bailey's leash and start snapping my fingers.

"So, Parker," he begins. "How are you?"

"Oh my God." I give in to the eye roll. "I'm fine, Jake. How are you?"

"I'm good. Getting used to St. Peter's and stuff."

"Why bother? You'll just be leaving soon anyway."

"I believe in making the most of my time," he says. We head farther down the street. "It hasn't been easy. I used to go to a public school and now I'm stuck in your stupid uniforms. And the praying drives me crazy."

"You and everyone else." I stop snapping my fingers and cross my arms. It's chilly out. "Do you know how much harder it is to become popular when you have to wear a uniform? You can't rely on being fashionable to help you climb the social ladder. Becky and Jessie and I had a hell of a time working our way up in those things."

"Tragedy," Jake says.

"Definitely," I agree. "Were you popular at your old school?"

"Would you like me less depending on my answer?"

"Jake, I don't think I could like you any less," I assure him. "Besides, I know you were. Popular people give off pheromones only other popular people can pick up on. Chris really took a liking to you, so I put two and two together."

"My best friend was the most popular guy in my old school," Jake admits. "His name was Adam Jenkins."

I don't say anything.

"I didn't necessarily want it," he adds, like that'll make me think more of him. "Why did you want to be popular?"

"Who says I wanted to be popular?"

"Please. You just said you worked your way to the top. Why?"

"Why does it matter?"

"I'm curious."

"You should really do something about that." I take Bailey's leash back. "I thought it would be easier."

Jake nods like he understands, but popularity is always different for guys—way less maintenance involved. It really *is* easier for them. And besides, I'm totally lying anyway. I didn't want to be popular because it was easier; I wanted to be popular because in high school that's the best thing you can be: perfect. Everything else is shit.

We keep walking and I wish he'd leave. Being on this street feels wrong. All these people, the cars flying back and forth—it's like a scene out of a movie and I belong to it with Jake and the dog. It probably looks perfect to someone watching from the outside, but it really freaks me out, so I keep glancing up and down the street, hoping for an opportunity to ditch him. And that's when I spot this familiar face outside Al's Convenience Store and everything stops. Like time. Everything.

He looks terrible, gaunt. Even from across the road, I can see the hollows of his cheekbones, and he's slouched over and pale and his hair's longer than he'd ever let it grow last year, like really long, like hanging-in-his-eyes long, and I don't understand why he's back. Why is he back and how soon before he leaves again?

"What are you staring at?" Jake asks, following my gaze.

"Becky."

I grab her by the arm and pull her away from her group of parasite-girls, the ones that live to bask in her reflected popularity because they haven't got a hope in hell of being popular themselves. It's funny because that's who Becky used to be.

"What the fuck, Parker?" She wrenches her arm from my grip and takes one look at my face. "This better not be about Chris or that stupid cheer, I'm warning you. You'll be thrilled to know we're not doing it—"

"Becky, shut up. Is Evan back?"

"Evan?"

"Yeah. Is he back?"

She stares at me.

"Goddammit, Becky, did you forget to turn your brain on today?"

"Don't talk to me like that!" At least she knows when she's being insulted. Chris sidles up and snakes his arm around her waist. "I don't know if he's back or not."

She's so useless. I press Chris's math binder into his free hand.

"Thanks," I tell him. "Hey, do you know if Evan's back or not?"

"What was that?" Becky asks Chris. "Why did Parker have your binder?"

"It's just math homework, Becky," he says vaguely. "Is who back?"

"Ev-an," I say slowly, and Chris gets this surprised look on his face—his eyebrow goes up and everything. He didn't know.

"*Evan?* Haven't seen him. Have you seen him?"

The lightbulb goes on over Becky's head.

"You let her copy your math homework?!"

She totally screeches it. I've always had the worst urge to tell her about how we used to make fun of her at the squad sleepovers she couldn't make. We'd up our voices nine octaves and say the most inanely stupid things because that's Becky for you. She was the most expendable member of the squad and now she's, like, Parker Lite.

She owes her magical senior year to me and she knows it.

"We're not supposed to be enabling Parker like this!" Becky says. What an ingrate. "That's what Grey and Henley called it—enabling! She uses you and you get nothing in return—"

"Oh, he got something," I assure her.

"Parker, shut up—" Chris turns bright red and since he's one of those people who like to make sure they do everything to the best of their abilities, especially the stupid stuff, he blows it: "You weren't supposed to say anything!"

Becky does a quadruple take and figures out what that means to the best of *her* abilities. She's probably decided we've had sex. Close enough.

"Fuck both of you," she spits, and storms off.

Jeez. Chris closes his eyes and brings a hand to his temple.

"So anyway," I say, "I was just walking down Victoria Street yesterday and I think I saw Evan outside of the—"

"Shut up, Parker," Chris says, strained. "Just shut up."
He chases after Becky.

We come downstairs looking like two people who've spent the last thirty minutes having sex. Chris insists on it because the basketball team has to know he's getting laid, so his hair is sticking up all over the place and the buttons on my shirt are strategically undone. Like any of the wasters on the team will notice, never mind the fact it's going to be the first thing he tells them.

The house is filling up with people from school. I spot a few girls from the squad, but they won't look at me because of what happened at practice earlier.

Chris grabs some of his buddies and gets to work on the tunes. In the minutes before the sounds of the latest popular white rapper start playing, I wind my way through the house and spot Evan in the kitchen, already working on some shots with Jenny Morse, who is not his girlfriend. This wouldn't matter if they were just doing shots, but after he passes a slice of lime to her they start kissing.

I clear my throat and they part fast.

"Parker," Evan says nervously. He runs a hand over his prickly black hair and holds out a bottle of vodka and a shot glass. "Uh—shot?"

"All students will proceed to the auditorium for a special assembly." Henley's voice crackles over the PA. "All students to the auditorium for a special assembly."

"Hi," Jake says, sitting beside me. For a second, I'm reminded of Bailey. "This is about the missing girl, isn't it?"

"What was your first clue, the mounted picture onstage?"

We are, in fact, skipping art for an assembly about the missing girl. There's a mounted picture of her onstage next to the podium, which is waiting for Henley. Rows of hard plastic chairs have been halfheartedly arranged in the center of the room and I've chosen a seat near the back and Jake has chosen the seat next to it.

This is the second assembly we've had for Jessica Wellington since she disappeared. First we pray to Jesus and ask him for her safe return, next Henley says a bunch of nothing platitudes, then Jessica's friends take the mic and share their favorite memories of her and then we pray again and then we're dismissed. Student Council hands out white ribbons in Jessica's honor at the door, so we never forget.

I look around the room. The auditorium is filling quickly. Everyone's talking in quiet voices on their way to their seats. Something about it makes me feel queasy.

Too many people.

"Chris is really pissed at you," Jake says. "He won't say why. What'd you do?"

"Nothing."

I inhale. How can the auditorium be only half-full and have all the air gone from it like that? I'm not getting any air. As students continue to mill into the auditorium, it gets smaller and smaller and my heart beats this insane rhythm in my chest. I rub my palms on my skirt. They're sweaty. I really can't breathe. No, I can.

I just think I can't.

Everyone's in. The teachers line up on either side of the walls, ready to shush us should the need arise. The lights overhead dim, but the stage remains bathed in an eerie golden glow. I take a few short breaths in and bring my hand to my chest because I'm afraid my heart is going to pop out of it. The tips of my fingers are tingling.

I close my eyes.

"Are you okay?"

I ignore Jake and exhale. Breathe in. Breathe out. That's

how you take care of these things, isn't it? In. Out. Again. Slowly. I've read it. Deep breaths. But what do you do when there's no air? When you're sucking in everyone else's stale breaths?

What if I really *can't* breathe?

"Wait, this is a test, isn't it? And if I ask if you're okay, it's because I have a thing for girls who are all vulnerable because they make me feel like I'm supermacho, right?"

I stand up so fast the back of my chair flies into the knees of the person behind me. They throw whispered insults my way and Jake stares at me, surprised. Henley strides across the stage and I stumble past Jake and down the row of teachers, some mangled explanation about having to go to the bathroom falling off my lips. And then I finally, *finally* burst through the doors to the hall and when I take that first breath in all I can think is *air* because I'm dying for it, gasping for it, and I can't stop.

Henley's voice floats into the hall.

"I've called this assembly today to pray for Jessica Wellington's safe return home. As more time passes, I know—as you all know—the outcome seems grim. But there is something else I know: If we put our hands together and appeal to God, we have a chance. *She* has a chance."

I end up on the floor, resting my head on my knees and trying to block out Henley's voice while I wait out my frantic heartbeat.

I focus on taking even breaths in and out.

"Wow. You're actually not okay."

"Would you quit stalking me? It's creepy."

I force myself up and brush off my skirt. In. Out. In. Out. My heart is starting to feel more normal, which means it's going away. Good.

"Sit down if you need to," Jake says. "I won't hold it against you. And I'm not stalking you. Grey told me to see if you were all right. It wasn't one of the most subtle exits ever."

"I'm fine," I mutter. "It's like some kind of claustrophobia. When I'm in a room with a bunch of stupid people like you, I get a little overwhelmed—"

"How were you *ever* popular?"

"I don't know."

"Do you want me to get Ms. Grey or a teacher or something?" he asks, awkward. "Or walk you to the nurse's? What do you usually do when you have a panic attack?"

"That's not what it was," I say quickly, but he's skeptical. "Just forget it. I'm going to skip out on the assembly. Tell Grey I have really bad cramps, okay?"

Jake makes a face. "Gross! I'm not telling her about your feminine problems—"

"Don't be such a coward!" I snap. "Just do it and your chances of getting into my pants increase tenfold."

I turn my back to him and start down the hall.

"Hey, wait! It'll be lunch soon! Am I gonna see you in the gym?"

I think of Becky and Chris glaring at me from opposite ends of the court and I don't have the energy to deal with that right now.

"No."

Later that night I find myself at Chris's again, except this time, on my way to the woods, I somehow manage to knock the top off this cement bird fountain and the sound it makes when it hits the driveway is awful. I dart out onto the street and I never look back, but I swear I hear Mr. Ellory open the front door and shout, "Who's there?"

nine

Chris and Becky are still furious with me. They won't look at or speak to me and, I won't lie, I feel pretty accomplished about it. Somebody give me a gold star.

Word around the halls is they're not totally broken up yet, just on a break. And I suspect word around the halls is I had something to do with it, because nothing else explains the dirty looks I'm getting from the cheerleading squad and the basketball team.

I guess that means I've almost arrived.

"So I was looking at the Honor Roll plaques," Jake is saying. Art again. He's making amazing progress on our landscape, and wouldn't you know it, he's actually kind of gifted at this drawing thing. I'm still tracing the same rocks. "And you know what name kept showing up? At least for the last three years?"

"Hmm." I pretend to think about it. "Parker Fadley?"

"Not only that, you were on the Honor Roll *with distinction*. What does that mean? I've never been on the Honor Roll before."

"It means I was better than perfect."

"And modest. Must've worked pretty hard to get there, huh?"

"I worked my ass off."

He nods and goes back to filling in the ravine with his pencil. A couple of minutes pass and I wonder what he's getting at.

"That's it?" I ask. "Aren't you going to ask me what happened or how I went from top to bottom in such a devastatingly short amount of time?"

"Were you really making out with Chris in the change room? And that's why he and Becky are on a break?"

"Maybe," I say. "Hey, that wouldn't be why Chris isn't in art today, would it? He's not off somewhere crying about it, is he?"

Before Jake can answer, a burst of static and white noise fills the room. Everyone quiets and the secretary's voice explodes over the PA.

"Mr. Norton, would you please send Parker Fadley down to the guidance office?"

"You heard that, Fadley," Norton says. He gives me this look like I've done something wrong, but that's okay, since it *is* the only reason I ever get called down to the office anymore. "Get down there."

I grab my books and make my way out of the room, Jake's eyes on me as I go.

"It's not Friday—"

I stop talking as soon as I enter the office. This is unexpected: Grey and Henley are sharing space behind Grey's desk and both of them look superformidable.

But even more unexpected than that is Chris.

He's sitting in a chair in the corner looking so guilty I know I'll have to kill him when this is over.

I force a winning smile at all three of them.

"What's the occasion?" I ask.

"Sit down, Parker."

Henley and Grey say it in unison, but judging by the looks on their faces, they don't mean to. I shoot myself in the foot and laugh. They both frown at me and I sit. Chris stares at his shoes. I ignore the knot in my stomach. I'm a great improviser, but I generally prefer having an idea of what I'm getting into.

Grey starts us off: "Parker, do you have any idea why you're here?"

It comes to me like that: the math homework.

"No, ma'am." Pause. "Ma'ams."

Henley stands. She never wastes time, ever. She may have told my parents she was wholly committed to getting me back on the right track, but she has a school to run. I can trick Grey into chasing her tail, but Henley I can't trick into doing anything.

"Mr. Ellory has informed us you copied his last unit's worth of math homework—homework you were supposed to have completed on your own." She rests her hands on the desk and leans forward, nearly elbowing Grey in the face. I have the sense not to laugh this time. "Homework Mrs. Jones was generous enough to grant you an extension on to complete. *On your own.* What do you have to say for yourself, Fadley?"

I concentrate on not blinking. I hear that's a sign of weakness.

"Well, what's Chris's punishment?"

His head snaps up. "*My* punishment?"

"I just did what everyone expected me to do," I tell him. "You're the one who's not supposed to enable me."

He starts spluttering.

"Now, just a minute here," Grey breaks in with that watery voice of hers. "What Parker means is—"

"Enough." Henley's voice is as hard as her face. "Fadley's right, Ellory. You're not supposed to be enabling her and I speak for Ms. Grey and myself when I say we're disappointed in you. However, given the nature of your relationship with Fadley and her penchant for manipulating people, the fault does not entirely rest with you."

Chris exhales. That's when Henley focuses on me.

"Parker, everyone in this room is on your side. You're a smart girl; you know that. Did you really think you'd get away with this?"

I can't believe someone as smart as Henley would be stupid enough to ask that question.

"Obviously, I did," I say.

"Don't get smart with me—"

"But I am smart; you just said it yourself." I'd better quit while I'm ahead. "Look, I wouldn't have done it if Chris hadn't offered. It's all his fault for giving me the option."

Chris sits up. "If I hadn't, you would've found someone else—"

"Oh, really? Like who, Chris? I find it pretty fucking amazing—"

"*Language,* Fadley!"

"That you're sitting here acting like a victim of my calculating mind considering what I had to do to *get* that math homework—"

"She came to school hungover!" Chris blurts out before I can tell everyone he used his homework to get my goods. This is so great.

Grey and Henley stare at me.

"When was this?" Henley asks.

"He *thinks* I came to school hungover," I say.

I will kill him.

Grey looks all disappointed. "Oh, Parker. Did you?"

"He *thinks* I came to school hungover," I repeat. "And besides, what I do in the privacy of my home is my business. You can't penalize me or take away my diploma for anything I do on my own time, in my own house, outside of—"

"But if you're caught drinking at school again, you *will* be expelled and you won't graduate. You know that," Henley says sharply.

Yes, yes, yes. I know that. I know that. *I know that.* I bite my cheek and nod, my chest tightening. I want to snap my fingers, but I won't do that in front of them.

I won't.

"Which brings us back to the issue at hand: copying Chris's math homework." Like I said, Henley doesn't waste time. She paces in the narrow space behind Grey's desk. "I only have one question, Parker. Why?"

"Well, it's not like I didn't try to get caught up."

It's not a total lie. There were a few nights where I stared at the homework and considered doing it. That should count for something.

"It's like every day I get further behind, no matter how hard I try to catch up, and it's all I can think about because I actually *do* want to graduate, but when I sat down and tried to do that stupid math unit it seemed so impossible, it made me want to kill myself."

It figures the last thing I should say is the first thing out of my mouth. The room gets so quiet I can hear the faint sounds of the chemistry teacher shouting formulas all the way down the hall through two closed doors. Henley stops pacing and glances at Grey, and Chris looks like I've slapped him across the face.

"Ellory," Henley says. "You're excused."

He forces himself out of the chair and looks all sad because of what I've said. I'd feel bad about it, but it's technically his fault I said it in the first place. As soon as he's gone, I put on my best *sorry* face, because this has the potential to get way out of hand.

"I didn't mean that," I say. "You don't need to call my parents."

"We have to call your parents now," Grey says.

"You said anything I say in this room is totally confidential, so we can trust each other! Don't you want me to trust you?"

"You'll never trust me, Parker."

I guess Grey's not as stupid as I thought or she looks.

But I can't let her do this.

"You *can't* tell my parents."

"*Enough,*" Henley says again. The bell rings. "Ms. Grey, call her parents; arrange a meeting. In the meantime, I'll be discussing what to do about this math situation with Mrs. Jones. Go eat lunch, Parker. You're excused."

Chris is waiting for me at the end of the hall when I come out. I maneuver my way around students on their way to the caf to get to him.

"I can't believe you told them even after I made myself *kiss* you!"

"I can't believe you said you wanted to *kill* yourself!"

"I wouldn't have said it if you hadn't *told!*"

"I *didn't* tell!" Chris yells. People stare at us. He grabs me by the elbow, drags me down the hall and pulls me into an empty classroom. As soon as the door is shut, he turns to me. "Becky told."

I cross my arms and wait. He looks nervous.

"Because she was mad at you, because of what we did—"

"How come she wasn't in the office with us?"

He shifts.

"*Chris.*"

I have perfected the way to say his name when I want information he doesn't want to give. I hit exactly the right tone, frequency, whatever, and it never fails: he caves.

"She told Henley and Grey she was afraid of you because you're so . . . volatile, and then she cried until they let her go. But you can't blame them for believing her and—hey! Where are you going?"

I hate her. I hate her. *I hate her.*

My feet walk me to the gym at top speed while a terrified Chris follows ten paces behind and I keep thinking about my parents. *My parents.* I don't even want to guess what I'll have to sit through when I get home.

I am going to *end* Becky Halprin.

I push through the gym doors so hard they *whack* against the wall. The basketball players—Jake among them—stop playing and the cheerleaders' heads snap up.

"Becky!"

I storm across the court. Becky stands, all white-faced and wide-eyed. She smooths her skirt and moves to meet me halfway. When I'm close enough and she's close enough, I reach out and shove her.

Hard.

"Holy shit," one of the basketball players says behind me.

The other members of the squad flank Becky instantly, but it doesn't matter. I only needed to shove her once, put the fear of God into her, that sort of thing.

And like I'd rob myself of the opportunity.

"Parker, don't," Chris says. I ignore him.

"I just realized it must really suck to be you," I say. "And it's all my fault."

She raises her chin defiantly. "What are you talking about?"

"I was a better cheerleader; I was a better cheerleading captain; I was a better student; Jessie liked me better; Chris liked me better; hell, Chris *likes* me better. How must that feel? How does it feel to know that even at my worst, you're still not enough?"

"Fuck you." She turns this hideous shade of red and her hands start shaking because the truth hurts. "Parker, I could make your life seriously miserable from where I'm standing."

"Becky, you're only standing there because I decided I didn't want to."

"Holy *shit*," the same basketball player repeats behind me.

I clear my throat.

"Parker," Evan says nervously. He runs a hand over his prickly black hair and holds out a bottle of vodka and a shot glass. "Uh—shot?"

Jenny Morse flees from the room. I take the bottle and the glass.

"Wow," I say. "This is so interesting."

I move to the kitchen counter, pour my first shot and knock it back. It burns going down and I have to make a concentrated effort not to choke. Chris says it's pathetic that after three years of high school I haven't mastered the taste of alcohol.

Chris says I should loosen up.

"You and Jessie made it up yet? Because she feels terrible about what happened at practice and she wants to make it up with you."

The words tumble out of Evan's mouth and I can't tell if he's lying. I pour my second shot, which is really stupid because it's not even dark out yet and it's the kind of thing I wouldn't let Chris get away with.

Evan watches. Hesitates.

"You're not going to tell her, are you?"

I shrug. He takes the vodka from me and pours himself a shot. Knocks it back. Then another. And another.

"I can't believe you," I say, reclaiming the bottle. I don't even bother to pour a shot this time, just drink it straight. It's gross, but Chris says I should loosen the fuck up. "I thought you loved her."

"Oh my God, I do," he says desperately. "Seriously, look, Jenny doesn't mean anything to me; she's just—"

"She's just a lay, right?" He doesn't say anything. "I knew it. I totally knew it. I had a feeling and I was right. I'm always right."

He's sweating now. "You're not going to tell her, are you?"

"I haven't decided yet."

I leave him there. When I step into the foyer more and more people are arriving and Chris has the music going proper, really loud. It's in my feet, up my legs, in my lungs, my heart.

The party has begun.

"Do you want to go to the mall with me?"

Jake glances over his shoulder. "Are you talking to me?"

He's such a dork.

"Yes, Jake, I'm talking to you."

"Me? Go to the mall with you?" He frowns. "Why?"

I don't have the patience for this.

"Because it's fun! I don't know, why do people go to the mall? I just thought since I was going to the mall after school and you're practically stalking me all the time, you'd probably wonder why I didn't get on the bus and spend all night obsessing over it, and I don't want to be responsible if *you* don't get a good night's sleep."

"You're having a rough day, aren't you?" he asks. "Everyone's talking about what happened at lunch."

I inhale slowly through my teeth.

"Look, do you want to go to the mall with me after school or not?"

"Uh, yeah!" Finally. He forces a smile. "Sure."

"Meet me outside after the bell."

There.

I've decided to kill as many hours as I can at the mall because I don't want to go home and face my devastated parents right away and I know the phone call from Grey will devastate them. Maybe they'll send me to an actual therapist or something; I don't know. I just don't want to go home until I absolutely have to, even if it does make everything worse, and I figure toying with Jake will be a good distraction from that eventuality, because I need that, too. A distraction.

"So why'd you ask me to come with you?"

The outside light and fresh air is immediately swallowed behind us as we step through the doors of the Corby Shopping Center. It's crowded, but I can stand being around this many people. It's not like school, where everyone knows me.

"Why not ask you?" I shrug. "Where do you want to go first?"

"I don't know. This is my first time at your local mall. Give me the grand tour."

"Well, we simply must start with the food court. Does international cuisine interest you? The first slice of pizza is on me."

"Just a sec." Jake reaches out and feels my forehead. "Temperature's normal. Invasion of the body snatchers, maybe? Have you been possessed? Remember, like, two days ago when you told me I didn't have a chance with you?"

I brush his hand away. "First slice of pizza is on you."

We don't have pizza, we have Chinese food and Coke on

Jake at my insistence, but I think he's the type of guy who would pay anyway. The food court is really packed, so we have to eat at the fountain. We sit on the edge of the pale pink tiles while water gushes out of the mouth of the large metal fish behind us. Loose change scattered over the bottom of the fountain catches the weak light overhead and glints at us. Annoying elevator Muzak is piped in from God knows where, but hey, it's a mall.

We're quiet at first and then I start thinking about my parents again, which I don't want to do, so I try for a conversation. A nice one.

"Tell me about you," I say.

Jake takes a sip of his Coke and stares at the shoppers passing by.

"What do you want to know?"

"Anything. Tell me about your family and life at your old school and—I don't know—what's the worst thing you've ever done?"

He laughs at that last bit.

"Uh, my dad is Earl, my stepmom is Wanda and my stepsister is Carrie. Carrie's in her first year of college, so she's not around." He thinks about it. "My dad works in tech support and Wanda does voice-overs for commercials. Pretty neat, huh? She's good, too. My mom's a zoologist. She lives way on the other side of the country."

"How come you don't live with her?"

He shrugs. "I had to choose. I don't have a problem with my mom; I just have more in common with my dad. No big deal."

That probably means it's a big deal.

I take a bite of a chicken ball. It tastes like paste.

"So what's the worst thing you've ever done?"

"I don't know."

"That must mean you're a good person."

"Define 'worst.' Are we talking academically, socially? I cheated on every single history test I had in the ninth grade. Socially—being popular is pretty bad, isn't it?" He cracks a smile. "I let my friends get away with things I couldn't live with if I'd been the one that did them. Or maybe I shouldn't be able to live with the fact I let them get away with that stuff, who knows?"

"What kind of things?"

"I don't know. What's with this question, anyway? What's the worst thing *you've* ever done? That's why you asked me, isn't it? So I'd ask you. I'm getting a handle on you, Parker."

"Why do you like me? I know you like me or you wouldn't put up with me or bother me as much as you do."

That shuts him up. But not for long.

"If I knew exactly why, I'm pretty sure I'd talk myself out of it." He clears his throat and looks away. "I don't know if you know this, but you're not the most personable . . . person."

"And you like me."

"Is this going to end with you telling me I'm never getting into your pants?"

"Even after what you saw in the gym today?"

He forces himself to look at me and he's totally embarrassed. I can tell this is really hard for him and I feel sorry for him because it's really complicated and stupid when you can't even figure out why you like a person—especially a person like me—but everything inside you is telling you that you do. It's not like I ever gave him a reason.

I just wouldn't want to be him right now.

"Maybe you like trying to figure me out," I suggest. "So maybe I should tell you what my deal is. Get it out of your system."

"Maybe I like trying to figure you out because I like you

against my better judgment." He pauses. "Or maybe if I figured you out, I'd like you more."

"I don't think so."

We stare at each other. I sense the kiss coming before he
actually leans in, and because I'm anticipating it, I get all
anxious and I start pulling at the tips of my fingers because
I don't know what else to do. His face gets closer and closer
and then I lose grip of my index finger and my elbow rams
into his Coke and spills all over the floor. The kiss never happens. I scramble for napkins and sop up the golden-brown
liquid.

"Were you raped?"

I stare at him. "*What?*"

He's *really* uncomfortable now. "I've been trying to figure
out why you're as fucked up as you claim you are. Is that
what it is?"

"No." I bend down and grab the empty cup. "No, I wasn't
raped."

The city bus drops me off two blocks from home. It's dark
and cold out and I make it a slow walk, even though I'm
tired and want to sleep. When I pass Chris's house, I notice
a small sign on the lawn that wasn't there before. It's planted
in front of the walk and has an air of authority despite its
size. I crouch down and read it.

PROTECTED BY LETHAM'S HOME
SURVELLIANCE AND ALARM SYSTEMS

I feel like I'm going to throw up. I can't see the cameras from here or the little strips of laser light that sound the
alarm as soon as you trip over them, but I know they're there
and just like that, I can't go into the woods anymore.

I force myself up. Close my eyes. Open them. I'm outside my house, at my front door, and I'm trying to figure out how to open it because this is the moment I've been dreading and my fingers aren't working right.

After a second I get it.

I'm not inside two seconds when Bailey runs at me, barking happily. I pat him on the head. The dog who's decided to love me no matter what I do.

"Where have you been?"

Mom and Dad pussyfoot into the hall from the kitchen. I know they want to look scary and parental, but they just look pale and scared. And devastated.

"Where have you *been*?" Mom repeats. "Your guidance counselor called us this afternoon and told us you were talking about *killing* yourself?"

"Now, Lara," Dad says quickly. "She did say she didn't think Parker meant it—"

"It doesn't matter—*you don't go around making jokes like that!*"

She loses it for a second. Her face crumples and she cries and Dad wraps an arm around her. Bailey paws at the carpet nervously.

"Lara, calm down—"

"Where *were* you?" She sniffles. "You know you have a curfew and you break it on the same day you're making *suicide* threats? Do you know what went through our heads when we got that call? We got you a dog, we thought you were doing better, you were doing your homework and now you want to *kill* yourself?"

They stare at me, waiting for an answer.

"I was at the mall," I say. "And now I'm going to bed."

"*Jim*," Mom says.

Dad steps in front of the stairs, blocking my path.

"Now just a minute, Parker. We're not finished here. What

were you *thinking*, talking like that? Is this something we should worry about? I mean—" He squints, like he doesn't know who he's talking to. "If it's going to be like this, maybe we haven't been doing enough. Maybe we should get some *real* help here—"

"*No!*" Bailey scampers to the living room for safety. I count to three. "I'm doing my best, but you just need to back off a little, that's all. Everyone does. Just leave me alone, okay? That's what I want."

Mom reaches into her pocket for a Kleenex and blows her nose.

"And then what? You do whatever you feel like? No curfew? You run off to another motel two hundred miles away and end up in the hospital again—"

I really don't want to hear it, but she won't shut up, so I force my way around Dad, head to my room and slam the door as hard as I can. After a minute, I open it and call for Bailey. He comes barreling up the stairs and down the hall and I sit on the bed and pet him. As tired as I am, I'm too wired to sleep now because all I can think about is that chintzy seventies-style wallpaper at that motel, the last thing I saw before I closed my eyes, and when I opened them again the walls were white. Hospital white.

Because I had my chance and I blew it.

ten

On Thursday, I sit through a meeting with Henley, Grey and my parents.

A few things are decided.

Instead of having to suffer through an entire math unit, I'll sit for a special test and we'll consider me all caught up and isn't that *great*?

Friday meetings with Grey are still on.

Henley shares Chris's concerns that I might have come to school hungover that one time, and I don't confirm or deny it.

I don't say anything at all, actually.

Mom and Dad fall all over themselves apologizing for the trouble I cause.

The school is too good to me, they say.

I don't think they realize how it sounds.

Friday, after history and before art, I find my name on the Honor Roll plaques hanging in the entrance corridor. Right at the top. Three years running, with distinction.

My parents used to love to tell everyone the story about

the time I was in kindergarten and the whole class was col-
oring these pictures of flowers and every time I went outside
the lines I demanded a new picture to work with. I was going
to do it *right* even if it killed me. Fifteen attempts later, I had
the best-colored picture of everyone. I still remember being
hurt when the teacher made as big a fuss over my classmates'
lesser efforts as she did over mine, which was perfect. Or
maybe not as perfect as I thought.

Talk about your self-fulfilling prophecies.

"Parker? Is that you?"

The air leaves my lungs. This horrible feeling settles in
the pit of my stomach and I decide I'm in school, but I am
dreaming this. And then I turn really, really slowly and everyone else in the hall disappears. I'm not dreaming it.

Evan.

He stands before me, still as pale and thin as he was the
day I saw him, but at least he didn't know I was there then,
and now he's here in front of me and I can't speak. He pulls
me into a hug and I feel his bones poking through his shirt
and I think I'm going to be sick and—*God, let me go.*

He lets me go.

"Oh my God, Parker, it's so good to see you." He brushes
a few strands of ratty black hair from his face. "How are you?
Chris called me a couple times and he told me—I mean, are
you still hanging in there and everything?"

I try to swallow, but my throat is totally closed and my
mouth is unbelievably dry. I can't believe how long his hair is
now or how awful he looks this close up.

My palms start sweating.

"Holy *fuck*!" a voice cries behind me. "*Evan?* Is that *you*?"

Chris and Becky hurry down the hall toward us and I
think that means their "break" is over, but that's hardly sur-
prising. Becky would never give up the most popular guy in

school that easily. Her face darkens when she spots me, but she forces a smile and lets Chris drag her over by the hand.

"Oh my God—how've you *been*?"

Evan laughs and Chris gives him one of those jock hugs, one of those violent squeezes that end in a brain-rattling pat on the back. I expect Evan to break. He doesn't.

"I can't believe this! Parker said she thought she saw you the other day! How long are you here for? Is it temporary? Are you going back to your aunt's or—and what the fuck happened to your *hair*?"

"Grew it out, man," Evan says, laughing self-consciously. Becky bounces up and throws her arms around him. They hug for a long time and I can see him breathing her in. I try to breathe in, but I can't. "God, Becks. Wow. You look great."

"So do you, Evan."

I can tell she doesn't mean it. And I know what she's thinking. She can't believe this is the guy she used to throw herself at all the time and he was always fending her off. Chris makes a few more exclamations of disbelief.

"So are you back?" Becky asks.

Evan shifts from foot to foot and smiles tentatively.

Oh no.

"Uhm, maybe. I mean, yeah. I had the time away that I needed and I've got an appointment with Henley and we're going to talk about me finishing out the year here. If I get the good-to-go, I'm coming back."

Chris whoops and claps his hands together and my head feels like it's going to burst and I can't breathe, so I just walk away from them and head to art. I'm the first person in the room. Norton isn't even here. I sit down at my usual spot, gasping. Get a grip, Parker. Just forget it. In. Out. The bell rings. Students start filing in. I bolt from my seat and wander over to the supply closet and pretend I'm looking for something. If I can do this to myself, I can make myself stop. It should be easy. Stop.

I'm coming back.

"This is humiliating."

"Trust me, this is hardly humiliating," the school nurse—Mr. Grant—says, as he takes my blood pressure. "And I can tell you about humiliating. You wouldn't believe some of the things I've seen here. This hardly registers."

"It was pretty funny, though," Jake says from his spot by the door. "Never pegged you for the swooning type."

"Fuck off. Why are you still here, anyway?"

"Hey now, enough of that." Grant gives me a hard look. "Okay, Parker, question time: did you eat breakfast today?"

I sigh. "Yes."

"But isn't crabbiness a sign of low blood sugar?" Jake asks. "No, I know what it is! It's okay, Parker; don't be ashamed. You're not the first victim of my dashing good looks. Girls take one look at my sexy face and it overloads their circuit boards. Should you write that down, Mr. Grant? She was looking at me when it happened."

Grant ignores him. "That time of month?"

"Agh!" Jake covers his ears.

I roll my eyes. "No."

Grant asks a slew of personal questions while Jake's ears are still covered, so that kind of works out. When Grant's finished, he fixes me up a Dixie cup full of water.

"So it's just one of those things," he says. Jake uncovers his ears. I nod and the lunch bell goes. "I want you to stay here until lunch is over and we'll see how you feel then." He turns to Jake. "Can you stay with her?"

I shake my head while Jake nods his head.

"I can do that," he says.

"Good. I'll be back shortly. I have to inform Mrs. Henley of this, Parker. They keep pretty good tabs on you, you know."

I stare into the Dixie cup. "Lucky me."

As soon as Grant's out of the room, I set the water down, head for the sink, grab a swath of paper towels, wet them and work on getting the yellow paint out of my uniform. Of course it wasn't enough for me to just pass out in class—I had to take a jar of yellow paint down with me.

"Maybe you should just sit for a second," Jake says, watching as I furiously scrub my skirt. The paint had better come out.

"I don't need to sit."

"I was joking before. It wasn't actually funny," he says. "I think you scared the hell out of Chris. Norton didn't know what to think."

I wish he'd stop talking. The paint isn't coming out. I toss the sopping towels into the sink and kick the cupboard underneath it, leaving a black shoe mark in the wood.

This is so stupid.

Jake stares. "It's not that bad, Parker."

I don't even want to dignify that with a response, but I do give him a look he shrivels under. I breathe in. At least I can breathe in now.

"My—" I head back to the cot and sit down. I can't bring myself to look at him. "My skirt didn't—it didn't, like, go *up,* did it?"

It takes him a minute to register that.

"You didn't flash anyone."

"But you do look like shit," a familiar voice says. Chris.

I flop back on the cot.

"Where's Becky?"

I make sure to say it in a supersnotty voice, hoping it'll make him leave faster.

"Cheerleading practice." I can't believe he hasn't given up on her yet. He studies me and frowns. "I had this funny thought while I was coming down here and now I have to know: is this about Evan?"

Jake looks from Chris to me. "Who's Evan?"

"He's—" Chris stops abruptly, backs halfway out of the room and glances down the hall. "Henley's coming."

I groan. "Someone *please* put me out of my misery."

The sound of Henley's high heels clacking along the floor momentarily precedes her, and when she enters the room she's got this look that says it all: she is tired of seeing my face. The feeling is so mutual.

"I heard what happened in Mr. Norton's class," she says. "Drinking in class again?"

"No."

"You wouldn't be lying to me now, would you, Parker?"

I cover my face with my hands. No one says anything. I hate that Jake and Chris are hearing this because it's none of their business and Henley should know better. I bite back the urge to tell her to do her job *right*.

"She wasn't, Mrs. H.," Chris says. "I mean, not that I could tell."

"Gardner?"

"It was—" He stops. I uncover my eyes while Jake gets all sincere on Henley. "It was an anxiety attack. I didn't see her drinking."

I know he thinks he's doing me a favor, so I try not to death-glare him.

"An anxiety attack?" Henley repeats. I can't tell if she's disappointed or not. "Well . . . that's something you can talk about with Ms. Grey on Friday, Parker." Thank you, Jake. Thank you *so* much. "Now if you'll excuse me, I have to get back to the teachers' lounge."

I snort. I bet they keep the good booze there.

Henley reads my mind and glares at me, but she goes.

"So it was Evan," Chris says thoughtfully. He laughs, kind of. "Jesus Christ, Parker. When do you think you'll stop kidding yourself, huh?"

"Oh, fuck off, Chris."

"Who's Evan?" Jake asks again.

I lie down, turn my back to them and stare at the wall.

"Just this guy we know," Chris "explains." "Anyway, I'd better get to the gym. Becky's waiting for me. Are you coming, man?"

"I told the nurse I'd stay here with her until he got back."

"All right, well. See you guys later."

"Chris, wait—" I sit up. "Since when do you have an alarm system? I saw the sign on your lawn."

He blinks, surprised.

"Some jackasses broke my mom's favorite bird fountain."

"You got an alarm and surveillance system for that?"

He shrugs.

"Dad's been looking for an excuse for ages."

Exit Chris. Jake turns back to me.

"Who's Evan?"

I stretch and yawn.

"Anyone ever tell you that you have a one-track mind?"

"Do you want some more water or anything?"

"No."

"So who's Evan?"

I gesture for him to come close. He hesitates.

"It's okay," I say. "Just come here."

He crosses the room slowly, and when he's close enough I reach out and grab his hand. He tenses. For someone who supposedly likes me, you'd think he'd be over the moon because I'm touching him, but no, he's suspicious.

I turn his palm up and trace my index finger over what I think is his life line. It's alarmingly short, if you believe that sort of stuff, and I don't. His breath catches in his throat. I hear it. I'm just fucking with him.

I let go of his hand and pat the spot beside me. He sits.

"I could like you, Jake." I can't believe I'm saying it. "But the more you know about me, the less interesting you become."

I'm not so steady on my feet. It's fifty minutes into the party and too much of the vodka is gone, and if I walk without leaning against the wall I'm afraid I'll do something dumb like fall over in front of everyone. Apparently my overwhelming fear of looking sloppy and stupid in front of the entire school is not as drunk as the rest of me. Next time Chris tells me to loosen the fuck up, I'm going to tell him to fuck the fuck off.

And I haven't seen Chris since he got the music going. I make a mental note to talk to him about that—it's too loud. The beat makes the house rock back and forth, or that could be the vodka, I don't know. I inch my way down the hall. I'm going to hide out in his parents' room and die on their bed. Someone can resurrect me in the morning.

"There you are!" Chris yells. Great. I turn really slowly and after a second the rest of the room turns with me. "I've been looking for you."

I give him a closed-mouth smile because I'm afraid to talk. "Hmm?"

"Let's go outside; the music sounds awesome out there," he says. "We can start off the poolside dancing."

"Uh . . ." My mouth is total sandpaper, thick. "Well—"

"Uh, well," Chris says, imitating me. "Don't think about it; let's go!"

He pulls my hand. I reach out for the stair banister to my left.

"Go without me." I think I sound okay. "I'm going to stay . . . here."

"What?"

"Go; just go," I say slowly. Maybe he can't understand me. I can understand me. "Without me. Poolside dance. Without me. Go."

He stares at me for a good minute.

"Parker, are you hiding something from me?"

"Uh—well." I swallow and let go of the banister, but the room lurches to the left and I have to grab it again. "No. . . ."

"Okay," he says. Phew. Then he grins. "Parker, you're drunk."

"I'm—" so not in the position to deny it, so I give him an accusing glare. "You told me to loosen up."

He laughs. For, like, five minutes he just stands there laughing at me.

"Not funny!"

"It is so!" he insists. "You know what this means, don't you?"

I shake my head.

"It means it's now my responsibility to make sure you have the most amazingly fun drunken time of your life or I'll never hear the end of it." He grabs my hand again and pulls me down the hall. "Come on! Poolside dancing!"

"No, Chris—" I dig my heels in. "Chris."

He turns. "What?"

"I don't want anyone to see me like this. Let me hide out in your parents' room, please—"

"You are the most sober drunk person I know." He says that like it's a bad thing. "Relax. It's a party.

In another hour you're not going to be the drunkest person here. Becky will be. No one's going to think less of you."

"But I'm cheerleading captain."

"So what? Come on; the fresh air will make you feel better."

He says it with such authority I let him drag me outside.

"Besides," he adds, as we step through the door, "I won't let you do anything really stupid. Look at it this way: it could be the best night of your life."

I look up. The sun gets in my eyes.

Everything goes white.

eleven

"I think we should talk about what happened yesterday," Grey says, squinting at me over her Parker notebook. I wonder what she's written about me so far and hope it's something lost cause-y. "Tell me what got you so upset."

I press my lips together.

"Did someone say something to you?"

I keep my mouth shut.

"Maybe I didn't give you enough credit when you told me you felt overwhelmed. Maybe none of us did. I'm sorry, Parker."

If she seriously believes *that's* going to get me to talk, I'm kind of offended.

She sighs.

"Is this how it's going to be?"

I glance at the clock and watch the minute hand snail forward. If I wasn't so committed to this silence, I'd say something like, *I don't trust you, remember?*

———

"Uh, what are you doing?"

"What does it look like I'm doing?" Jake asks, settling into the seat beside me. The bus jerks forward. "I'm sitting beside you."

"No, you're not. Your seat is in the middle. Nice try, though."

He has the audacity to ignore me, sets his book bag on his lap and rummages through it. After a minute, he pulls out a folded sheet of paper and hands it to me.

I unfold it. "A love letter? How sweet."

"No." He turns pink. "It's just something I found on the Internet—"

"Porn? You shouldn't have."

"Just shut up for five seconds. It's breathing techniques, to get a handle on your anxiety. I thought you might find them helpful." I stare at him and he turns even pinker. "You know. So you don't pass out in class again—"

"I got it, Jake. About five sentences ago."

I know a thank-you would probably be more appropriate, but what happened yesterday continues to humiliate me, so never mind. I guess he can sit here just this once.

"Anyway, we've really got to start thinking about our art project," he says. "A lot of people have already started painting. We should probably be doing that."

"Got any ideas?" I ask. I don't. I barely think about our project when we're in class working on it, let alone out of class, on my own time.

"Not a sweet fucking clue." And then he rushes headlong into what he says next: "Do you want to brainstorm together at that coffeehouse on Victoria Street today, after school? It looks really good. I've wanted to try it ever since we moved here—"

"Are you asking me out?"

He blinks. "Am I?"

I lean my head back and stare at the bus ceiling where a huge wad of pink gum has attached itself. Gross.

"Well, say you *are* asking me out. That means you'd have to get off at my stop and we'd go from there, right?"

"It seems that would be the most convenient way to go about it."

I unfold the paper in my hands. *HOW TO BREATHE*. I fold it back up again.

"You'd have to meet my parents," I say carefully. "I've sort of freaked them out lately and they don't really like me going out when I can't be supervised, and since they've never met you they'd probably say no *and* I'd probably have to be back before my curfew, which is seven thirty. . . ."

I look him directly in the eyes.

"I mean, you know how it is. You chase a bottle of sleeping pills with a bottle of Jack Daniel's and life's never the same, no matter how many times you try to tell people it was an accident."

"Is that a no?" he asks. "If you don't want to, just say so. You don't have to be such a smart-ass about everything."

I want to laugh, but I don't. There's something unsatisfying about what just happened here. I set the paper down.

I could have a good time if I went out with Jake. But that doesn't mean I should.

"*Are* you asking me out?"

"Yeah," he finally says.

"Mom, Dad—this is Jake Gardner."

After they get over the initial shock that I still have a friend to bring home, my parents play twenty questions with Jake. They're straight out of The Parent's Handbook and they're so standard it doesn't even matter who's asking them.

MOM/DAD: Well, it's nice to meet you, Jake! Gardner, Gardner . . . that wouldn't be any relation to the Gardners down on Marriott Avenue?

JAKE: Thanks, nice to meet you, too. It might be. See, my family just moved here from the West Coast not that long ago.

MOM/DAD: Oh, wow! How exciting! Welcome to Corby! So how do you know Parker? Do you two share a class together?

JAKE: We have art together. We're partnered for a big project due at the end of the year.

MOM/DAD: Oooh. Aaah.

At this point I go upstairs and change out of my uniform. When I go back downstairs, wearing something more casual, Jake and my parents are winding it up.

MOM/DAD: And your parents—what do they do?

JAKE: Well, my dad's in tech support down at that call center in Belton, my mom's a zoologist and my stepmother does voice-overs for commercials. You've probably heard her. She did the one for those crazy mop-broom hybrids. The Bop?

MOM/DAD: My mother-in-law *loves* the Bop! Wow! That's great, Jake! You're welcome here anytime!

We decide not to go to the coffeehouse right away, opting

to wait for the school day to settle first. And Bailey needs a walk, so we take him to the dog park.

"Here, Bailey." Jake grabs a stick off the ground. Bailey hops around lightly as Jake swings it back and forth. "Fetch, boy!"

Jake throws the stick. Bailey goes lunging after it and lets out a startled yelp when he's jerked back by the neck, and that's when I realize his leash is wrapped tightly around my hand at a painfully short length.

"Shit!" I say. "Oh, Bailey—I'm sorry!"

He gives a pitiful whimper and I crouch down and gesture him forward. He tiptoes up to me with this big Sad Dog expression and it makes me feel guilty. I wrap my arms around his neck because I don't know how to apologize to a dog, but this one always wants me to pet him, so a hug should be, like, huge.

"I'm sorry, Bailey. I didn't do it on purpose."

"You're obviously unfamiliar with the game of fetch," Jake says behind me.

I ignore him and pat Bailey on the head until he looks less pained and more adoring and for a second I think I'm going to do something I haven't done—and genuinely meant—in a long time.

Cry.

Chris is crying over my hospital bed the second time I wake up. The first thing I think is I can't pay him back. It's the first thing I say, too.

"Good boy." Bailey wags his tail. I turn to Jake because I can't shake this stupid sad feeling in the pit of my stomach. I snap my fingers. "Do you think he hates me for that? I mean, do you think he understands it was an accident?"

"He's a dog," Jake says. But then he looks at my face. "But sure, yeah. I bet he understands. He's clearly smitten with you."

"Clearly," I echo. I shove my hands in my pockets. "You have a lot in common with my dog!"

"Har, har," he says, reaching for another stick.

"I don't feel comfortable letting him off the leash," I say quickly, and Jake drops it and then I start feeling even worse for some reason. I shouldn't be doing this with him. I should stop. "And I'm not hungry. We should skip the coffeehouse."

His face falls. "Sure, that's fine."

"But we can still do this, though," I say.

"What's this?"

It's a good question. We're just standing here, Bailey sitting between us and glad to do it, but it's not really anything and Jake wants something. So I think about kissing him, but then I don't because that would be really stupid.

"I guess I'll just catch the bus home then, is that it?" he asks. "I wish you'd told me you weren't really into this, Parker."

"It's not that—"

"Then what is it?"

"Never mind. Let's just go to the coffeehouse."

He laughs. "Right, yeah, we'll just do that when you've already said you don't want to. You know, this is so typical—"

"No, I do! I asked you if you were asking me out and you said you were and I agreed to it, so we're going to eat and we're going to talk about our stupid art project, okay? You cancel a date before it happens, not during. So we're going to the coffeehouse. That's what we're doing."

"Fine, Parker. Whatever."

We drop Bailey off at home and go to the coffeehouse and I order a bagel and a black coffee and Jake orders a chicken salad sandwich and a black coffee and neither of us says anything even though we're supposed to be talking about our art project.

"If I knew why you liked me," I say after the waitress

drops the bill on the table, "I could probably handle it a lot better."

"That makes two of us." He hesitates. "Do you even like me at all?"

"I don't know. It freaks me out. I try not to think about it too much."

Jake sighs, grabs the bill and stands. I do the same. And then I start thinking of the dog and I feel guilty all over again and I want it to go away and snapping my fingers doesn't help, so I do that really stupid thing.

I lean over the table and kiss him.

twelve

Chris wants to talk.

In homeroom, he hisses my name, but I ignore him. In art, he tries to start a conversation and I ignore him. After the bell goes, he tells me to meet him in the gym and—ignored. He either knows about Jake or wants to talk about Evan and I don't want to talk about either, so I have to find somewhere else to spend my lunch hour, somewhere that's relatively peaceful and not totally crowded.

Like the chapel.

Why didn't I think of it before? If I'd thought of it before, I never would've tried the nurse's office or made a habit of "hiding out" in the gym. The chapel. It's only a Catholic school. No one goes to *the chapel*.

But I'd forgotten just how awful and uncomfortable the place makes you feel until I push through the doors and step into the little God's House adjacent to the caf. It's like the walls know I'm a bad person. I stand before the altar, cross myself—force of habit—and try to pick the best pew of the lot, settling for one in the middle on the left-hand side. I could sleep away my afternoon classes and no one would ever think to look for me here.

"Parker?"

I groan.

"Oh my God. It's true."

"Go away," I mutter. "I'm not talking to you."

"You're a mess."

The thing about being drunk is people want to congratulate you for it, often in the form of giving you more to drink.

Or maybe this anomaly is only true of people in my high school.

Chris drags me out to the pool and for the next hour all anyone can talk about is how Perfect Parker Fadley is actually drunk, and then they slap me on the back and they say "way to go" all admiringly, and next thing I know, someone's pressing a red plastic cup into my hand. And because I start feeling that rush I usually feel when I've done something perfectly and everyone knows it, I drink whatever is in the red plastic cup.

And then I get props and another red plastic cup.

Four or six red plastic cups later, I have:

Danced horrendously in front of everyone, even though Chris assures me I looked sexy and plenty of guys want to "tap" that, nearly fallen into the pool, told several people I loved them, apologized to most of the cheerleading squad for being a Dictator—except for Becky—fallen down and cried, was helped up and laughed, threw up, cried again, told Chris I hated him for doing this to me because I was being stupid and he promised me I wouldn't be and stumbled away to the front lawn, which is where I'm lying now, flat on my back with perfectly manicured blades of grass pressing into my legs, hands and neck.

Chris is probably searching for me all over the house and backyard where the party is, which is why I'm out front, where the party isn't. The remaining minuscule sober part of my brain refuses to let me make a fool of myself in front of everyone any more than I already have and the remaining minuscule sober part of my brain says the only way I can do this is if I stay the fuck away from people altogether.

"Do you need help up?" Jessie asks. "If I get Evan and Chris and maybe Becky, I'm sure we can drag you up to Chris's parents' bedroom."

I throw my arm over my eyes.

"Go away."

She doesn't. She sits down on a patch of grass close to my head.

"Still pissed at me over what happened at practice, huh?"

"Go." I uncover my eyes and give her my best death glare, which I'm pretty sure is totally compromised by my total drunkenness. "Away."

She smiles. "Nope."

"I work really hard!" I struggle to sit up. "And you made a fool of me—"

"You made a fool of yourself by having a brain aneurysm in front of the entire squad," she interrupts. "You should've seen your face. You were going apeshit over the stupidest things, like, oh my God, we missed the beat. We'll get it. We always do."

"I wasn't having a brain aneur-an-any—" She laughs. I want to kill her. "Thing."

"And Chris is worried about you," she says.

I groan. "Shut up."

"He actually came to me; that's how worried he is. He's afraid to talk to you. He thinks you're fixing for a breakdown because you're, like, obsessed with perfection." She says this as breezily as someone relating the weather. And then: "So I told him about the panic attacks."

My heart stops. "You didn't."

She leans over me. Her face blots out the sky, and a strand of long blond hair hangs in front of my face, tickling my nose. I turn my head.

"It's the end of the year, Parker. Things are supposed to be winding down."

She makes me tired.

"Give Becky captaining duties until the year's over," she continues. "She's always wanted to do it and you can let her and say you did something nice. I've talked to the squad; they said if you do that, they'll want you back next year—"

This sobers me up completely for about five seconds.

"No. Are you out of your mind? Becky will do the loser cheer and we'll be a laughingstock—"

"It doesn't matter! Everyone hates you right now. You're an anal-retentive control-freak perfectionist and they need a break and so do you. And so do I—I can't do damage control for you anymore!"

"They only hate me until they give the best performance of their lives thanks to me and then they love me!"

She snorts.

"That's true and you know it," I mutter. Everything spins and I close my eyes. "I'm that good."

"Yeah, and the sooner you make a mistake and learn to live with it or let them make mistakes and *learn to live with it, the better. Until that actually happens, I really think you're going to give yourself a stroke. You're not responsible for everything, Parker. You can't control the way things end up. Stop trying."*

"Then it's my fault either way. Me, them. Everyone knows I do everything, so if they fuck up, it's my fault, and if I fuck up, it's my fault and—" I can barely think the words before I say them and start losing my thread. "The way it is, that's good. I'm a good person because it's the outcome that matters and I always do things that are right in the end—and that's how you get away with being a control-freak perfectionist, because in the end you're right . . . and there's no excuse for anything less. I am not going easy on them—"

"I'm getting Chris. You are so wasted it's unbelievable."

And she's right, but only about that. I'm right about everything else. A second later, I feel her brushing a strand of hair from my face. I push her hand away.

"Go, please. . . ."

"Look, Parker, I'm telling you this as your best friend. You're freaking everyone out. If you don't step down, I'm going to do everything I can to get you off the squad for your own sake, and Chris has agreed to help."

It takes everything, but I push myself up from the ground and pitch forward. Jessie grabs me by the elbow and helps me regain my balance, but I don't want her help. I jerk my arm from her grip and fumble sideways, reach out, rest one hand against the side of the house and wait for the world to right itself.

This is cheerleading. Serious business. My reputation's on the line and, and, and they know . . . they know I'm not—

"*I can't believe you went behind my back.*"

"*Parker—*"

"*Evan's cheating on you with Jenny Morse. They're fucking.*"

I slide down the side of the house until I'm sitting. Jessie looks like she's underwater, wavery, discombobulated, but I can still make out her expression: openmouthed, white-faced, hurt. I didn't want to tell her like this, but she deserves it. She shakes her head, totally shocked, and marches past me so she can break up with Evan, give him hell, ask him if it's true, whatever. I don't care.

"*I'm only telling you this as your best friend,*" *I call after her.*

"Parker?"

The voice comes as a total surprise.

Maybe if I stay really, really still she'll go away.

"Parker, I know you're there. I can see your feet."

I heave a colossal sigh and sit upright.

"This is unexpected, Becky," I say. "What do you want?"

She marches up the aisle in an annoyingly self-assured way, a brown paper bag clutched in one hand, and sits beside me.

"Chris has been going crazy trying to talk to you, but he said you're avoiding him. So I said I'd talk to you because I know you won't avoid me. And we should probably talk, shouldn't we?"

"What about cheerleading practice?"

She shrugs. "Postponed."

"I never postponed for anything."

"This is important."

"So self-sacrificing," I sneer. "I bet it really turns Chris on. I bet he's thinking it won't be so bad being your boyfriend after all. Actually, I know he's thinking it. And so do you. That's the only reason you're here."

She inclines her head, like we're playing chess and I made the first move and it wasn't a bad one.

"I really wanted to start over with you after everything happened. I thought it was possible." She stares at the wooden cross mounted to the wall. "For about five minutes, I almost felt like there was this mutual respect thing going on. . . ."

I laugh. "While you were wasting time feeling things, I was stealing your *Beowulf* essay and passing it off as my own."

She clenches her jaw. "At least after *I* saw Evan I didn't lose it."

"I'm disappointed. That's the best you can do?"

"Yeah, it is." Becky nods. And then she nods again, like she really means it. "You know who feels sorry for you? Chris. That's pathetic."

"Yeah, it is pathetic that he's still in love with me."

She rolls her eyes.

"Do you feel sorry for me?"

It's one of those questions I ask before considering whether or not I really care about the answer. Who am I kidding? It's Becky. Of course I don't.

"You've made a choice and it's so obvious. I see it; I accept it," she says. "Even if no one else can. You want to rot and I want to let you."

If I was feeling generous, I'd congratulate her. The only person standing in the way of ultimate popularity—me—had stepped aside and she snapped up the position before anyone else even realized it was available. She probably watched me all year, waiting to see how my calculated fuckups could benefit her, and figured out my motivations in the process. That takes talent.

"Who would've thought that you of all people would be smart enough to get me?"

"Yeah, weird, huh?" She hands me the bag. "Consider that my contribution."

I peer inside of it. "Becky, if I'm drunk in school again, I'm expelled. I still want to graduate."

"Do you really?" She stands and stretches. "I'd better go. Chris is waiting for me. Is there anything you want me to tell him?"

"Nothing I wouldn't tell him myself."

She heads back down the aisle and I stretch back out on the pew, holding the paper bag to my chest, the bottle of Jack heavy inside it. The door creaks as Becky opens it and I wait for the click, the noise that tells me it's closed and I'm alone again, but it doesn't come. And then, her voice:

"You know, it's not any harder on you than it was for the rest of us."

thirteen

"Uh . . . what are you doing?"

"What does it look like I'm doing?" I ask, settling into the seat beside Jake. The driver shifts gears, the bus shakes and our shoulders bump. "I'm sitting beside you."

"No, you're not. Your seat is at the front," he says. They say imitation is the sincerest form of flattery. I'm so flattered. "Nice try, though."

It's weird sitting in the middle of the bus, but it's my peace offering to Jake for flaking out on him since the kiss. By "flaking out" I mean I may or may not be avoiding him or ignoring him outright when he talks to me, unless it's something to do with our art project, and then I wait, like, five minutes before responding, which I decided last night wasn't very nice of me.

"I'm not moving," I tell him.

"Evan—" He clears his throat. "Evan is Chris's best friend. He left before senior year because he had a breakdown or something. Chris told me."

"Very good, Jake," I say, nodding slowly. "And can you tell me why he had a nervous breakdown?"

"Nope."

"Well, if you can't tell me that, you can at least tell me what any of it has to do with me," I say.

"Chris said he'd tell me what everybody already knows," he says. There's an ungodly pause because we both know what's coming next. "You *did* try to kill yourself."

"It was an accident."

"Oh, right." He doesn't believe me. "That's why you meet with Grey, isn't it? And that's why no one leaves you alone and you're not popular anymore and Evan fits in there somehow. That's your big secret, right?"

"Congratulations, you figured it out. So how 'bout them Mets?"

He blinks. "What?"

"Does every conversation between us have to be like this, with you prying into stuff that's none of your business? So tell me: How 'bout them Mets? What do you think?"

"Oh, they're just great," he mutters. "So are you depressed—"

I groan. "Jake."

"Okay, okay," he says quickly. "Never mind."

"Do you think I'm depressed?"

"I think it'd explain the bravado."

"You think this is bravado?" I shake my head. "Actually, you know what? You're right. I sit at the front."

I grip the seat ahead of me and stand, but before I can step into the aisle, Jake reaches out and grabs my wrist. I give him a look that says, I don't have time for this.

"You kissed me," he says.

"So?"

"Would you please sit down? I want to talk to you."

I do it.

"Look, I'm sorry that you—" He doesn't finish and I'm

glad because he'd only embarrass us both if he started apologizing for something he knows nothing about. "Why did you kiss me if you were just going to shut me out after?"

I shrug. "Had to fill the moment at the coffeeshop somehow."

"Ouch."

"You were expecting something more?"

"Yeah, I guess I was."

"Why would you do a stupid thing like that?" I chew my lip. "The way you feel about me freaks me out. I've told you that."

"Maybe the way *you* feel about *me* freaks *you* out."

"But I don't know how I feel about you. I try not to think about it. And I've told you *that*."

I guess he knows I could run us in circles forever, so he leans in and gives me a kiss, all soft and hesitant, and I think it's supposed to make my heart beat faster and my head feel lighter, but it doesn't. It steals my breath and makes the tips of my fingers tingle and I start thinking I'll have an anxiety thing again, here on the bus while his mouth is against mine, and how awful that would be. A funny thought occurs to me at the same time Jake brings his hand to my face: I couldn't do this even if I wanted to do this.

"Stop telling Jake things about me."

Chris slams his locker door shut. "You're talking to me now?"

"Why did you tell Jake I tried to kill myself?"

He pretends to think about it. "Because you did?"

"I didn't." I rest against his locker. "That's what you think I did."

He does that lean guys do with their girls. I'm against his locker and he rests his hand just above my head and tilts forward so we're close. He doesn't even think before he does it; it's second nature. We used to stand like this every day between classes and he'd give me a kiss when the bell went. Sex is one thing, but I always thought that stupid lean meant intimacy. Because I was dumb.

"You drank a bottle of Jack Daniel's and downed a bottle of sleeping pills. I don't think you tried to kill yourself, Parker; I know it."

"You obviously know nothing and now Jake's getting the wrong idea about me."

"What do you care what Jake thinks about you?" He rolls his eyes. "Okay, you tell me what you think happened and if I think it has merit, I'll find him and clear things up. Sound fair?"

"I got drunk first," I explain. "And then I miscounted how many sleeping pills I needed to get through the night. It's hard to count when you're all fucked up."

"Well of *course!*" He slaps his forehead in disbelief. "That explains *everything.* How could I have been so stupid?"

"I'm serious. Stop telling Jake things."

"I don't tell him anything everyone doesn't already know. That's fair game." Chris finally becomes aware of the way he's standing and how close we actually are. He straightens and rubs his hands on his shirt. "He really likes you, huh?"

"I guess. Why do you think that is?"

"Damned if I know. That's not exactly the type of conversation you want to have with the ex. But I picked up on it, took pity on the guy and told him about that one time you tried to kill yourself."

It starts making sense. "You wanted to scare him away."

"No, I thought I'd let him take comfort in the fact that when you're fucking with other people, you're really just fucking with yourself. Becky and I had a talk about it and she threw that theory out there, and I gotta say it makes so much sense."

"Becky is becoming a real pain in my ass."

"Becoming?" Chris studies me. "You like him, don't you?"

"Would that bother you?"

"Even if it did, I've resolved not to let it ruin a good time with Becks."

"*Becks?*" I shake my head, disgusted. "But you don't love her."

He shrugs.

"You love me," I say.

He shrugs again.

"Oh, come *on*—this from the same guy who blackmailed me into kissing him in the change room because he missed me so bad? You've *never* liked Becky—"

"I didn't really know her before. And believe it or not, Parker, things happen around you that have nothing to do with you even if they start out that way. She's not that bad. By the way, Evan's back in two weeks. He has to get all his shit from his aunt's and cut his hair, but you should prepare yourself."

It throws me. I need a second.

"So he just cuts his hair and he's back?" I ask. "Everything's like it was?"

"Yeah, hopefully. Are you going to be okay? I worry—"

"Don't."

I head in the opposite direction, to my locker, open it and grab my English books. The bottle Becky gave me is sitting on the top shelf, face out, so everyone will see it, but no one sees it. I'd like Chris to see it. And I'd like him to ask me where I got it.

———

"Hey, Jake! Stop!" I manage to catch him between third and fourth period heading to whatever class it is he heads to. He waits for me to jog over.

"What's wrong?" he asks when I reach him.

I untie my ponytail and retie it. I'm not sure how to do this.

"I'm sorry," I finally say.

He raises an eyebrow. "You're sorry?"

"Yeah." I untie my ponytail again. "I don't know."

"You don't . . . know?"

"And even if I did, I wouldn't know how to say it."

"Parker, what are you talking about?"

My stomach twists. "I think you're okay, but I know you deserve better."

He looks totally confused now.

"You're making my brain hurt—"

"So now you can't say I didn't warn you."

He stares at me a long time. And then I see a light go on. Vaguely.

"Does that mean you—"

My stomach twists again.

"Don't call it anything yet," I say.

He nods slowly.

"I have to go."

I leave him in the hall and run to the girls' washroom, where I push through the closest stall door and throw up.

"You're like Jake in dog form," I tell Bailey after I mark the day Evan is coming back on the calendar above my bed. I sit down beside him and pet him. "I wish we hadn't gotten you."

Bailey gives me this uncomprehending, painfully loyal look.

"You make me feel bad," I clarify.

I reach for my math book, open it to the unit I never did and start reviewing. I have that test tomorrow and I need to pass it because I want to graduate, I guess.

I guess.

So I can get out. They can all leave me alone forever. Right.

I stare at my calendar. At that big red *X*.

"Wow."

Mrs. Jones looks up from my test, all startled. I insisted she mark it as soon as I scribbled down the answer to the last question and watched her eyes grow wider with every red checkmark. I'm not nearly so surprised; I stayed up all night studying like I used to. Sometime after midnight it became imperative to me that I show everyone I still possess those wonderful qualities that helped separate me from everyone else.

Because it makes the way I am now that much more frustrating for them.

Jones shakes her head in total disbelief as she scribbles a bright red *100%* in the upper right-hand corner of the paper.

"Congratulations, Parker."

"This demands celebration," Chris says, holding up the test and waving it around. Jake laughs and Becky gives a tight-lipped smile.

I rip it from Chris's hand. "It does not demand a celebration."

Suddenly, we're a group. Jake caught me outside of math, saw the test score and told Chris, who was with Becky, as we passed them in the hall. And here we are.

"You're right," Chris agrees. "I'm just looking for an excuse to party."

"Party?"

"Hang out." He chews his lower lip. It's what he does when he's thinking. He doesn't do it very often. "Why don't we all go to my house after school and watch a movie or whatever? My parents won't be home."

"Sounds good," Jake says.

"Because I got a perfect score on my math test?"

"If there's got to be a reason, that can be it," Chris says.

"Can't. My parents wouldn't like that." And for the first time in my life I'm happy to say this: "You know, because of my curfew and all. And it's a school night."

"Well, let's try them," Chris says. He pulls his cell phone from his pocket, dials my house and hands me the phone.

"Oh, fuck you," I say, pushing it away.

He brings it up to his ear.

"Hi, Mrs. Fadley? This is Chris. . . ." He pauses and winks at me. "I *know*, it's been way too long. . . . Yeah! I'm great. Yourself? . . . That's great. . . . Uh-huh—oh no, it's nothing like that. Parker's fine."

Becky and Jake stare at me. I pinch the bridge of my nose.

"I'm calling because a few of us are getting together at my house after school. We're going to watch a movie, that sort of thing. . . . Yeah. I was wondering if Parker could join us. She mentioned a curfew and it might be a little late by the time we're done, but I'd drive her home and—yeah, my parents will be home. . . . Uh-huh, yeah. Just a sec. . . ."

He hands the phone to me. I give him a death glare.

"Hi, Mom."

"Why couldn't you ask me that yourself?" she demands.

"I don't know. But I got a hundred percent on my math test."

"Are you being serious or are you joking?"

"I'm not joking. I can show you the test later tonight."

"You're not going to be drinking over there or anything, are you?"

"No, Mom. Chris said his parents will be there."

"Well, you know the Ellorys. They may be *there*, but they're not—"

"Okay, forget it. I'll see you after school." Yes.

"No, no, no," she says quickly. "Go and have a good time. I'm proud of you, Parker—for the test. And I didn't know you and Chris were still on speaking terms. That's good—these are good things. Go have fun. Your father and I love you."

I close my eyes. "Bye."

fourteen

I can't figure out what's stopping me from just ditching Chris, Becky and Jake and going home while they stand in front of the shelf full of junk food at Al's Convenience, trying to decide what snacks to get. Suddenly, we're a group. It makes me sick. I head over to the magazine rack and try to remember how to breathe and that's where Jake finds me ten minutes later, my eyes closed, snapping my fingers.

Breathe in.

"We've picked the eats," he says. Out. "Chris is paying now."

"Okay." In. I open my eyes.

He extends his hand, like for me to take, and when I don't, he drops it and it's awkward. That's what happens when you sort of tell someone it's okay if they've kissed you and it's okay if it happens again, but you don't tell them if it's okay to do couply things like hold hands and, I guess, care.

"Okay," I repeat. "Let's go."

"*Wait.*"

"Stop following me." Slam. *"I said get away from me!"*

I turn my head in the direction of the noise. It takes such an effort, I think I must be dying. I feel like it. I blink slowly, several times, until I can sort of focus on a pair of people silhouetted by the moonlight filtering in through the window blinds.

"Nothing is going on between me and Jenny Morse—"

"That's not what Parker said!"

I close my eyes.

"What? You're taking Parker's word for this? She's drunk off her ass! When we dragged her in here she was telling us what a beautiful person Becky is! I am not fucking Jenny Morse!"

"Oh, really? Because that's not what Jenny Morse told me and she wasn't drunk off her ass when she said it!"

She starts to cry.

"Oh, Jesus, Jessie. Don't cry, please. . . ."

"I can't even look at you right now. Get out."

"No, please, Jess—we can figure this out. I'm not leaving this room until we do. Don't do this. Please."

"There's nothing to figure out, Evan."

"What does that mean?"

Silence.

"I asked you what that meant."

"What do you think it means? I don't want you here. Get. Out."

All of a sudden I'm being jerked upright. My stomach lurches. I try to tell whichever one of them it is to stop and leave me alone, but I can't move my mouth.

"Parker, sit up. You can't stay on your back because if you get sick—" Jessie sobs and taps my

cheek, once, twice, three times. Stop. I want to sleep.
"Parker, come on."

"I hope she chokes."

"Nice, Evan. Would you just leave?"

"Not until you talk to me about this."

"If I talk to you about this now, I'll just say some-
thing that you really won't like—"

Their voices disappear and so does everything until
seconds, minutes, hours later, I don't know, Evan's
shaking me, grabbing me roughly by the shoulders.

I try to push him off me, but my arms don't work.
I think he's crying.

"—Because you couldn't keep your goddamn
mouth shut—"

"Jessie."

I open my eyes. I'm pressed up against Jake's left side and
the flat screen mounted to the wall is rolling the end credits
for the movie I didn't watch. I rub my eyes and straighten
up. Chris and Becky stare at me.

"Welcome back," Jake says.

"Trust you guys to pick the most boring movie on Net-
flix," I grumble.

"It kept the rest of us awake."

I lean forward, rest my head in my hands and try to shake
the sleep off.

"Who were you dreaming about?" Chris asks.

My eyes travel from him to Becky.

"Nothing. No one." I stand. "I'm going to get some air."

"Come back in soon," Chris says. "We're popping out the
bubbly."

"Really?"

"Coke's bubbly, isn't it?"

Becky giggles and rests her head against his shoulder. He
puts an arm around her.

I've never met a girl so content to be a growth.

Outside, I stand in front of the woods, but I don't go in. All I can think about is getting caught, the cameras that could be recording my every move, that memory-dream and Bailey's my dog and Evan's coming back and there's a bottle of Jack in my locker Becky gave me and Jake's allowed to kiss me and this isn't at all how things are supposed to be going. I wanted to be alone. It's safer that way.

After twenty minutes or so, I hear footsteps behind me.

"I've kissed Jake," I say.

"I know."

I turn and there's Chris, all washed-out in blue moonlight.

"He told me because he felt guilty," he explains. "I told him to go for it."

"I don't like you with Becky. She's not a very nice girl."

"I don't like you with Jake. He's not me."

"Do you remember that party at the end of junior year . . ."

I trail off and look up. The stars are out tonight, full force. They're pretty.

Of course he remembers.

"How could I forget?"

"I'm a different person now."

He regards me for a long time before he says, "No, you're not."

"Yeah, I am. I am so, so far away from all of that." I don't even know why I'm saying this. It just feels like I should. "It's all totally behind me."

"Whatever you say." He holds out his hand. "Let's get back to the house."

"She's nicer than me, though."

"Who?"

"Becky."

"Come on, Parker. Let's go in."

"Wait; I—"

I turn back to the woods before I realize what I'm doing. I didn't even get to—

"Are you okay?"

"No. What?" I want to shake myself. Stop looking over there; you can't go over there, so stop. I run my hand over the bracelet on my wrist. There's nothing else there that I don't have. "I mean, yes. I'm just tired. I was hard on you, wasn't I? I never let you get away with anything."

"Yeah, but you never let anyone get away with anything."

"You were worried about me."

"I worry about you."

"You know, even when I was really hard on people and not very nice, they always thanked me afterward because you couldn't argue with the results." I kick at the ground and give a bitter laugh. "Couldn't argue with perfection."

"You were running yourself into the ground."

"I didn't want anyone else's mistakes jeopardizing my track record. And God forbid *I* made a mistake. Because if it ever turned out wrong, what would that say about me? I mean, what would happen?"

"The world would end. You wouldn't even know how to cope," Chris says lightly. "And that's what did happen."

"No, it didn't." I shake my head. "That's what I'm trying to tell you: I'm not Perfect Parker Fadley anymore. I never was. I know who I am now and I'm more in control of my life than I've ever been."

"You're a perfect mess. You even have to do *that* perfectly."

"Look, I'm trying to tell you not to worry," I say impatiently.

"I'll do what I like." He sighs. "We should really go in."

Becky and Jake are talking happily when Chris and I return to the house. They each have a glass of Coke. Chris pours one for me.

"So," Becky says as we crowd around the island. It feels like those moments after everyone has left the party and before you start cleaning up. "Ms. Abernathy told me all these old cheers the squad used to do, like, way back in the day, so at the next game, we're going totally retro. Old-fashioned music, chants, everything. I think it'll be great, like nothing we've done before."

"What about the outfits?" Chris asks. "You're not going to go retro with those, are you? When Abernathy was a cheerleader the skirts went down to the ankles."

The guys laugh like Chris has told an amazingly funny joke.

"Oh, don't you worry, Chris," Becky says, touching his arm. "You'll be able to see our underwear."

I raise my glass. "Classy."

"I know." She eyes me. "What do you think, really? Think it's a good idea?"

I shrug. "Can't be any worse than the cheers you've been doing lately."

"I can't believe you were cheerleading captain," Jake says to me.

Becky smirks. "Cheerleading Dictator."

I set my glass down.

"Jake, walk me home? That way Chris doesn't have to get the car out."

So he does.

"It's nice out," he says, as we tromp down the driveway. "I mean, it's definitely getting warmer out."

"Yeah. . . ."

"My mom doesn't talk to me."

"What?"

"My mom doesn't talk to me," Jake says. "Because I chose my dad. He cheated on her with Wanda. I guess she thought I'd stay with her because of what he did, but I've always had more in common with him."

It's the kind of thing that interests me, but I don't want Jake to think I'm interested, so I swallow the million questions fighting their way up my throat until I can't.

We're pretty close to my house at that point.

"So do you forgive him?"

"Yeah, I guess so," Jake says. "I mean, he's sorry."

"Do you forgive your mom?"

"I didn't think I needed to."

"She should talk to you. You're her son."

"Yeah, but it's more a case of her having to forgive me, isn't it?"

"But are you sorry?"

He pauses. He looks sad. "No."

"Why are you telling me this?"

"Because . . ." He shrugs. "I don't know. Because I want you to know we've all got something?"

"Oh, Jake. You're so melodramatic and angsty."

"Yeah, we have a lot in common." He shoves his hands in his pockets. "Did you mean what you said before?"

"What did I say before?"

"The more I know about you, the less interesting I am. . . ."

"I guess not," I say. "Lucky you."

"Lucky me," he repeats. "I'm going to kiss you."

So he does.

fifteen

Something's not right.

I set my book bag down and listen. There are the usual sounds coming from the kitchen; Mom puttering around, getting dinner ready maybe. That's normal, almost welcome. But something's missing. Not right.

I round the corner. My perfect test is stuck to the face of the fridge, the way my childhood drawings used to be. Mom's gearing up to do the dishes, but Dad's not at his usual spot at the table.

And Bailey didn't run to greet me when I stepped through the door.

"Where's Bailey?" I ask.

Mom looks up.

"Your father had to take him to the vet."

"What happened?"

"He got into a fight with another dog at the park."

"Is he hurt?"

She nods. "He might need stitches."

"He's not—" I swallow. "He's not going to die, is he?"

She gets all hopeful around the eyes.

"Are you worried?"

Why do people do that? Turn nothing into something?

"I couldn't care less either way."

She flinches and turns back to the sink. As soon as I leave the room, she might cry about how much she doesn't understand me anymore, how much she wants her old daughter back, but she's not coming back. I went too far, but sometimes you have to.

"He's not going to die," I say.

But she doesn't look at me and Bailey comes home with stitches on his hip and a lampshade around his neck so he won't gnaw at them. I take pity on him and I let him sleep in my room.

"Are you going to the dance?"

I slam my locker shut.

"What are you talking about?"

"You know. . . ." Chris wiggles his hips in a poor imitation of dancing. "The dance this weekend. You going?"

"I'm not following."

He rolls his eyes, grabs me by the hand and drags me down the hall to the entrance corridor. There, on the wall, is a bright pink poster advertising the semi-formal this weekend. Be there or be square.

"There are only, like, a half a million of these all over the school," he says.

"Semi-formal already," I say, staring at the poster. "How about that."

"So are you going or what?"

"Well, I *would*, but no one's asked me." I jut my lower lip out, but his eyes light up, so I drop the expression and snort. "Are you kidding me? Of course I'm not."

"I have it on good authority that Jake's going to ask you, though."

"Why does Jake insist on breaking his own heart?"

"Just go," Chris says, groaning. "I'm taking Becky. We'll all go together, leave together. It'll be fun times. Supervised fun times. How can you resist?"

"Easily. Contrary to popular belief, Chris, I don't like spending time with you, Becky or Jake. Especially Becky. In case you've forgotten, she annoys the fuck out of me. She's not a good argument for my going to the dance."

"So show her up!"

"What?"

"Wear that really nice black dress you've got, fix your hair up all nice and show her up. She'd hate that."

I can't help but laugh. "She *hated* that."

"There, see? I just gave you a reason to go."

"If Becky knew you said that, I don't think she'd like you very much."

"You won't tell her," he says. "And I think you should go."

"Why do you care?"

"Because I'm still in love with you, of course. What else could it possibly be?" Before I can say something snide, he laughs. "Haven't you done the whole Alienate Everyone thing long enough? I mean, how much longer are you gonna keep at it?"

"Uh, I don't know—until it works?"

"You used to like going to dances," he reminds me. The bell rings and we head for homeroom. "Bet you still do."

"I can't take this anymore."

"Can't take what?" I ask, even though I know.

Jake and I are so done with the sketching part of our

landscape, but because we haven't figured out what to do next we spend most of the period taking turns tracing the same set of rocks. I don't know why he's so freaked out about it. It sure beats working.

He gestures to the paper.

"Unity and disparity. We need a plan."

I rest my head on the desk. "Why?"

"Because that's the project!"

"Head up, Fadley!" Norton yells. "Nap time's not for another fifteen minutes!"

Everyone snickers. I raise my head.

"So-o-o . . . ," Jake says, and I can tell by the way he protracts the *o* he's getting ready to ask me to the semi-formal. Sure enough: "What are semi-formals like at St. Peter's?"

Why are guys so predictable?

"And what's a *semi*-formal, anyway?" he asks quickly, before I can answer his first question. "Does that mean dress nice from the waist down?"

"Something like that, yeah," I answer.

"Are you going?"

"I'm probably not allowed."

"That's convenient."

He stops tracing the rocks and I pick up where he left off.

"No, really," I say. "I'm not sure if I'd be allowed. I'm not even allowed off grounds for lunch, remember? Grey and Henley would probably have to okay it, not to mention my parents. It's not as simple as me putting on my best dress and going to the dance, you know?"

"And if it was?"

"It's not."

"Would you go to the semi-formal with me, Parker?"

I look up from my rocks. Chris is watching us from across the room. He winks and turns back to the landscape he's working on with his partner.

I hate him for enjoying this.

"Uhm." I focus on the rocks. "I guess."

"I'm twenty dollars richer, thanks to you!"

I shut the door to Grey's office and try to figure out what she's talking about. And then I roll my eyes. She just grins.

"The math test?" I guess.

"Principal Henley didn't think you'd pass, but I knew you would."

I lean against the door. I should be sitting so we can have our weekly session where I pick the lint off my skirt and determinedly maintain my silence while she stares at me, except today I have to break that silence. And all for a boy, too. How degrading.

"I want to go to the semi-formal tomorrow," I announce.

Grey blinks.

"What do your parents think about that?"

"They think it's a great idea."

She raises both eyebrows. "Really?"

"Call them and ask."

It's sort of true. Mom and Dad think going to the semi-formal with Jake and the gang *is* a great idea, but only because I've already told them it was okay with the school. I wait until Friday to spring it on Grey because I don't want to give her or Henley all the time they need to think up the reasons why it's probably not a good idea.

And they would, too, since the last dance I showed at was a disaster.

"Jake Gardner asked me," I continue. "They think it would be good for me."

"You don't have any plans to spike the punch again, do you?"

She gestures to the seat across from her and I sit.

"No. I'll just be there to look pretty and dance."

"I'll have to check with Principal Henley. This is very short notice, Parker—"

"But if you tell her you're okay with it, there shouldn't be a problem. Henley—*Principal* Henley's too busy to take a long look at a Pros and Cons list for my attending one semi-formal. You only have to give her the word."

"But I'm not too busy for that list." Grey smiles in a way that doesn't thrill me. "And we have thirty minutes of this session left. So how about you talk to me, *really* talk to me, and maybe you can attend the semi-formal."

"Ms. Grey!" My eyes widen. "That's dirty pool."

And it's really not worth spending an evening with Jake in an auditorium decked out to look like something special with a bunch of people I can't even stand being around on a good day.

But my parents think I'm going.

"Fine," I say, opening my arms. "Ask me anything."

She puts her best Movie Guidance Counselor face on and leans forward.

"How are you?" she asks after a beat. Oh my God. "How are you *really*?"

When I wake up, I'm still drunk.

I'll remember this as the longest, most miserable night of my life. Chris's living room is empty, no trace of anyone having been here, but the party is still going strong outside the door because it isn't that late, I just got smashed that early.

My shoulders hurt where Evan shook them. I hold my hand out. It feels like lead, but at least I'm not cemented to the couch like before, which is good because

I'm going to be sick.

I force myself off the couch, and fumble my way to

the door, trying to remember which bathroom is clos-
est to the living room while at the same time vowing
never to drink again because I've been here a million
times and I should know which bathroom is closest to
the living room, but my head feels awful and I just
can't think.

I push through the door and bump into God knows
how many people as I weave down the hall. Mostly
all of them laugh at me, or maybe they've just hit
the Feel Good Stage of the party where everything's
funny. Who knows. My stomach flip-flops.

I cover my mouth.

The closest bathroom is occupied and there's a lo-
ong line and there are three bathrooms upstairs, but
I don't think I'll make it to any of them in time. The
music is so loud it forces any other potential plans of
action right out of my brain and I stumble through
the kitchen, head outside, take a few uncertain steps
toward some bushes and throw up until there's noth-
ing left in my stomach to throw up.

And then I start dry-heaving, which is worse.

When it's over, I sit back on the grass, trying to
ignore the sour taste in my mouth and wondering how
I'll make it back to my safe haven in the living room.
And that's when I spot Jessie by the pool, Jessie
laughing it up with some guy I don't know. He looks
older than us and she's in full party mode, probably
buzzed, and the way she leans into him is all wrong
because it's how she leans into a guy when she wants
to fuck him. This is wrong. I did this. I focus on get-
ting upright again. I have to fix it.

"Parker?"

"I'm getting by," I tell her.

What else am I supposed to say?

"Well, that's good. Because things are happening, aren't they? Evan Corman is coming back. That must be nice for you and your friends." Grey's voice is like nails on a chalkboard. "I saw him when he met with Principal Henley. He seems eager to get things together. You two could help each other."

"How?"

"Well, given the circumstances . . ."

"You mean because he tried to kill himself, you think we can help each other?" I can't believe I'm sitting through this for a *dance*. "It won't help."

"Why not?"

"Because Evan didn't really want to die. And mine was an accident."

"Evan didn't want to die?" she repeats slowly. Stupid. "The evidence certainly suggests otherwise."

"He didn't," I say. "He planned it right down to getting caught."

Stupid, stupid. And then I decide to give it to her because when people are this stupid they should be told every once in a while.

"When he got in the bath with the razors, he knew his mom would find him before he bled out," I say impatiently. "It was more a gesture than anything. Like, 'This is how far I would go for absolution,' and everyone was like, 'Wow, fine, you're forgiven.' And that's how he lives with himself. He did his bit and he goes on like before. Which doesn't help *me* at all."

"And is this—" She makes this sweeping gesture around the room, like she's gathering up all the things I've done. "Is this your bit?"

God, she's so *stupid*.

"Look, can I go to the semi-formal or not?"

She stares at me a long time.

"Wait here."

She leaves the room. I sit in the hard plastic chair and wait, wait, wait for, like, ten minutes and then she comes back.

"You can go to the semi-formal," she says, shutting the door. "You can go to the semi-formal, but if you're on anything less than your best behavior—"

"I know; I know. I won't graduate."

"That's right. You won't."

The bell rings. I head for the door.

"Thanks," I say without looking at her.

"English homework," Becky says, handing me a piece of paper. I grab it and she heads on her merry way. "See you Monday or something."

"See you tomorrow," I call after her.

She stops, turns and gives me a hilariously quizzical look. It could be worth it for this alone.

"What?"

"I'll see you tomorrow. For the semi-formal? You, me, Chris and Jake." I force a big smile at her. "I'm really looking forward to it."

I'm such a bitch, but Becky makes it so easy.

sixteen

Hair.

I stand in front of the full-length mirror mounted on the back of my closet door and try to figure out what I'm going to do with my hair. Jake won't be here for another two and a half hours, but any girl knows you need at least three to look your best for a semi-formal. And I haven't even showered yet.

So I do that.

And then I stand in front of the full-length mirror mounted on the back of my closet door and try to figure out what I'm going to do with my wet hair.

Blow-dry it, probably. For starters.

So I do that while vaguely recalling a time I made checklists on dance nights. I reduced getting ready to a list of tasks, all of them allotted certain amounts of time for completion. As I checked off each one, I got to enjoy a warm feeling of accomplishment for an allotted 1.5 seconds.

But not tonight. The lack of structure disorients me. I decide to leave my hair down and curl the ends. While I wait for the iron to warm, I pick out my best black dress from the closet. It has off-the-shoulder short sleeves and stops just before the knees. Decent, but sexy, and miraculously uneaten by moths. I have a feeling it's not going to fit what with the ten pounds I've gained and the fact that I haven't done anything remotely physical since I quit the cheerleading squad, but unfortunately it does fit. Kind of. My boobs look desperate to break free of the soft satin material that binds them, and if I sit I have a sneaking suspicion the whole dress could split down the back. But if that happens, then hey, at least I'll have an excuse to leave early.

The dress (barely) on, I begin to work on my hair, which is a longer process than I'd like it to be or ever remember it being. It's because I don't have a list.

And the makeup. That's another beast entirely.

How did I do this every day for school? I didn't need a checklist then. The routine was so ingrained in me because it was so important because—*why?*

Because I had to look perfect, of course.

I pick through the collection of makeup on my desk. Foundation, under-eye concealer, lipstick, lip gloss, eyeliner, eye shadow, mascara and blush. I settle for clear gloss and mascara and then stand in front of the mirror and inspect myself.

It's good, I guess.

"Parker!" Mom shouts. "Parker, they've just pulled up!"

I grab my black clutch and hear Mom cooing all three of them into the house before I'm halfway down the stairs. I've barely stepped into the living room when Bailey comes bounding at me, lampshade tight around his neck.

"Bailey, stop!" I say before he can jump up. He comes to a screeching halt and I reward him with a pat because I can't help it, he looks that ridiculous. "Good dog."

"Look at that! You know, he doesn't even fetch my slippers

anymore," Dad says from his recliner, smiling. "You look beautiful, honey."

I bring my clutch up to my chest. "Dad, don't."

"Well, you do. Have fun at the dance." He gives me a look. "And behave."

"I wouldn't dream of doing anything but."

I give Bailey one last pat on the head and make my way into the kitchen, where Mom's having an animated conversation with Jake, Chris and Becky. She has the camera out. Joy. I clear my throat. They stop talking and look at me.

"Oh, Parker!" Mom cries. "This is the best you've looked in *ages*!"

Becky smirks, but not for long. We simultaneously ascertain that I look better than she does, even packing weight. Just because one has an affinity for pink doesn't mean she should wear it, but boy, is she. Pink hair accessories, jewelry, makeup, dress, shoes, clutch. It's one of those hard, bright pinks, too. Not the soft, pretty kind.

I mean it's blindingly awful and awfully satisfying all at the same time.

"I just want to get a picture of all of you, really quick! You look *so* nice!"

Mom ushers us into a line and places me between Chris and Jake, who both look very handsome. They've opted for black suits. Chris's hair is slicked back and Jake's is loose, like it always is. Chris smells like pine; and Jake, like paper. For a minute, I can't remember whom I'm supposed to be spending the evening with.

Jake.

Mom raises the camera to her eye and says, "Smile!"

"Thank God that's over," Becky says as we cross the lawn to Chris's car. She glares at me. "Your mom is such a freak, Parker."

"Well, I think it's sweet that she wanted to get a memento

of this grand occasion," Jake says cheerfully. "Your mom didn't take any pictures, Becky."

She snorts. Chris opens the driver's side door and gives me this look.

"I've seen that dress before," he says, letting his eyes travel over me. "But I don't think you've ever worn it quite like this."

I glance at Becky. She clenches her jaw, climbs into the passenger's side and slams the door shut. The night can only get better from here.

"I've gained weight," I tell him. "All in my boobs."

"Looks good on you," Chris says as he gets in the car.

Jake opens the back door for me. What a gentleman.

"You look really beautiful. I like your hair."

He says it in a voice I don't really deserve and it catches me off guard. I feel my face heat up and bring a hand to one of my curls. It's a weird moment.

"Thanks. You look nice." I reach out and push a stray piece of hair away from his eyes. "I like your hair, too. It looks very complicated."

We smile at each other and get in the car.

The dance has a ten-dollar entrance fee, the music is loud and bad and the auditorium is sparkly, purple and hot. Chris gives me a longing look as Becky drags him over to the popular corner. Just because we came together doesn't mean we stay together, especially when I look a thousand times better than Becky does.

And I get the feeling by the way everyone is staring at me that I look *great*.

Or a boob has popped out or my dress has split down the back.

I spin for Jake, just to make sure.

"Everything in place?"

"Do that again," he says, so I do. "Yeah, everything's in place. Now do it again."

"Maybe later, but only if you're good." I scan the room. Everyone's in various stages of bad-dancing to the bad song piped through the mega-speakers onstage. "I don't think I can dance the fast ones in this dress, Jake. Sorry."

"We could have one continuous slow dance instead."

"Now why didn't I think of that?"

"Because you can't see your chest the way I'm seeing your chest. It gives me thoughts. . . ."

I stare at him. "Feeling confident?"

"I'm matching wits with you or something."

He smiles and holds out his hand. I take it and we step onto the dance floor and make a mockery of slow dancing by pressing up close and swaying back and forth. I rest my head on his shoulder and think of Evan, who will be here soon, and what that means and I think of Grey and all the stupid things I said to her just to get to this moment.

He did his bit and he goes on like . . . before.

Have I done my bit and that's why I'm letting myself be here? The answer comes to me quickly: no. I can't lose everything I've worked so hard to give up. I'll have to make up any good parts of the night later. So I'd better enjoy myself while I still can.

I trace a circle on the back of Jake's neck with the tip of my finger.

"I want to have a nice time tonight," I say.

"Me, too," he replies, his voice cracking. I stop tracing. "But what's a nice night for Parker Fadley? Just so we're clear."

I have to think about it. "I won't say anything mean, you won't ask questions I don't want to answer and I might let you kiss me. You'll make me laugh at least once before the night is over, preferably by making fun of Becky. We'll dance and have punch and on Monday we won't talk about it."

"Okay."

"What about you? What makes a nice night for you?"

He leans his head back and stares at me. "Everything you said, but maybe you'll tell me something that makes me understand you better, or where I stand with you better, and I'd like to see where we are on Monday and go from there."

"Forget about Monday," I warn him.

"We'll see."

"Please don't set yourself up for disappointment."

"Be quiet," he says. "I'm trying to think of something disparagingly clever to say about Becky and I'm coming up short."

I laugh.

"Wait, does that count? I made you laugh! That counts!"

"You didn't make fun of Becky, though; you totally failed."

"She's a bitch . . . face?"

I bite the inside of my cheek. "Points for trying, I guess."

The fast dance stops and a slow one starts, but I'm tired of this, so I gently extricate myself from Jake, and we wander over to the punch, where he fills up two cups. We lean against the wall and watch Becky, Chris, their court and subjects try to turn a poorly decorated room into an event and I try to let myself feel happy because I'm not one of them anymore—but I'm not really happy about it tonight. I *did* used to like dances. I raise the cup to my lips and sip slowly. It's just punch. Boring.

"Nice bracelet," Jake says suddenly. "You always wear it. Was it a gift?"

"Uh . . ." I stare at the thin gold strand. "Yes and no."

And then my chest feels tight because of all the moments for him to bring it up, he'd pick this one. I snap my fingers, desperate to head off the bad feeling before it starts.

"Do you want to do something fun and not allowed?" I ask.

He eyes me warily. "And what would that be?"

I lead him around the edge of the dance floor. Grey, Henley and Bradley are clustered in one corner "supervising." They should be ashamed of how easily we sneak by them and find ourselves in the middle of the darkened halls, which is against the rules.

We have the whole school to ourselves.

"There's this rumor the skeleton in the lab glows in the dark," I lie. "I've always wanted to see if that's true."

Jake smiles. "Lead on."

The way our footsteps echo down the hall is pleasantly creepy. When we peer into the lab, Jake notes with a hint of sadness that the skeleton doesn't actually glow. Despite this, I open the door and step inside. I love the lab. The right wall is mostly made up of windows, big ones that let in lots of light. Moonlight, in this case.

Jake follows me in and shuts the door behind us. He wanders over and sits on top of one of the tables. I sit beside him— very carefully, so as not to break my dress—and swing my legs back and forth. It's quiet for a while, peaceful. I like that.

Then he speaks: "So I think I've finally figured out why I like you."

"Do tell."

"It's really unoriginal, but . . ." He clears his throat. "I've never met anyone like you before."

"Ah," I say. "You're right. That is really unoriginal."

"Well, I think you're—you're not nice. And you're definitely self-absorbed, but . . . you interest me." He pauses. "You know how when you meet someone and they just give you the impression they're living on this entirely different planet from everyone else? That's sort of how I felt when I met you. I thought, 'It must be something to know the girl who tells you that you want into her pants like five minutes after she meets you.' I mean, after I stopped being pissed off."

I force a smile. "And is it something?"

"It's difficult," he says. "You're very difficult."

"I don't mind you, Jake," I say after a second. "There. That's what you get from me. And you get tonight and on Monday you get nothing."

He stares at me.

"You really mean it, don't you?" he asks. "Do you think you're doing me a favor? Because—don't."

"I'm doing *us* a favor. Let's get it out of our systems."

"Why don't you just want to start something with me, seriously? Like maybe a date that doesn't end weirdly, like seeing a movie. . . ."

He runs a hand through his hair.

"Because this way is better," I tell him.

"But what if we did it and you found out you really liked me?"

"I could make myself get over it."

He winces. "Do you do that a lot?"

"Yeah, I'm great at it. And you're ruining this."

"Sorry."

And then he kisses me, just forces his mouth against mine, and I'm surprised by how rough it is, but that's fine, if that's how it has to be. I bring my hands to his face and press my fingernails into his cheeks hard, and he pushes me back against the desk and I'm lying down and some small part of me thinks this is funny; we're going to do it in the lab.

I reach down, push his jacket aside and fumble with his belt. Jake runs his hand up my thigh and nibbles my lower lip while I unbutton his pants. His fingers drift over my chest and his mouth moves down to my neck. I pause and enjoy the feeling of his lips against my skin. He's really good. And then he stops.

"What?" I ask. I'm short of breath; he's short of breath.

He leans back, but his face is still close enough for me to give him a light kiss on the lips. "Why are you stopping?"

He stares at me a long time and then he skirts off the desk, red faced, and starts buttoning and buckling up.

"I don't want to do this," he says. He doesn't sound like he means it.

"Yes, you do." I sit up.

"Not—not . . ." He takes a deep breath. "No."

"Why?"

"Because it's a bad idea," he says, tugging at the edges of his jacket. "Because I don't see Monday going all that well if I fuck you in the school's science lab tonight and pretend it never happened. Which is pretty stupid, since I have a feeling this was the closest I was ever going to get."

"You're right," I say.

He groans and rubs his eyes.

"You're so frustrating, you know that? You want everything and none of the—are you scared?" He shakes his head. "Is that it? I think we could have a great time."

"We could still have a great time—"

"Except forget it happened on Monday, right? And I can kiss you, but I don't know if I can hold your hand. And I can kiss you, but I can't ask you questions. Forget it, Parker. If you're too afraid to start anything, just forget it." Pause. "*Are* you afraid?"

I keep my mouth shut. We crossed a line here. Even if we didn't do anything, we really crossed a line. He sighs and opens the door to the lab.

"Whatever," he says. "We should get back."

I edge off the table but make no move to leave. I feel guilty. I hate that feeling. It's like when Bailey's looking at me and he loves me and there's nothing I can do to convince him he got such a raw deal being stuck with me.

"Are you coming?" He sounds impatient.

"I'm sorry," I say. I focus on the wall above his head because I can't look him in the eyes. "I had this plan before you got here and it's hard for me. I mean, I'm afraid—"

I hate being honest. It feels gross.

"Anyway." I swallow. "I am sorry."

It was supposed to be a nice night.

Sneaking back into the auditorium is slightly more complicated than sneaking out, but we manage. We head over to the uncomfortable metal chairs lined against the wall and sit down. It's hot, stuffy. I try and fail to spot Chris and Becky amid a throng of dancing students. Jake leans his head against the wall and closes his eyes.

The music goes fast, then slow.

"Want to dance?"

He opens his eyes. We're back where we started.

"Sure."

We dance. He wraps his arms around me and our foreheads touch and I decide this is the nice moment; this is what I'm allowed to have. I like the way he feels next to me, and if I were someone else I could be his girlfriend. And then I pretend to be her and tomorrow doesn't worry me; two weeks from now doesn't worry me. Everything is fine.

And then the dance ends.

When I get home, I realize the bracelet is gone. I imagine it slipping off my wrist in Chris's car, in the lab, on the dance floor, on the ride back.

I cut off my hair.

seventeen

Evan steps into the entrance corridor like a ghost.

People pass him without a backward glance, none of them aware of this new old addition to the halls of St. Peter's High. I watch—from a safe distance, of course—as he takes the school in like he's never seen it in his life. His hair is short, clean-cut like before, like Chris said it would be, but he's done nothing for his weight.

Leave.

I think it as hard as I can, but Evan's skull is so thick it'll probably never get through. Still. *Leave. You're not wanted here.*

I do not want you here.

My chest gets tight and I try to focus on all those techniques on the paper Jake gave me, but it doesn't work because I don't remember them, and besides, they'd never work. When my hands start shaking, I know I have to get away. I give Evan one last look and head in the opposite direction. So I can't be around him at all; that's fine. St. Peter's is a big school. I could avoid him easily for the next few . . . months.

The bottle in my locker is begging me to open it.

But I want to graduate. I want to graduate.

"I want to graduate."

I don't mean to say it out loud.

"What?" Jake looks up from our landscape. "What did you say?"

"I want to graduate. It's my new mantra."

"Oh." He turns back to the paper.

"No congratulations? It's a very positive mantra for me."

"Nope."

Things you can't do with someone without fucking up the weird enough relationship you already have:

1. Almost have sex with them in the school's science lab.
2. Give yourself a really bad haircut?

Actually, I'm not sure the haircut has anything to do with it. He hasn't said a word about it. Chris freaked, Becky laughed—she's finally better looking than I am—but Jake, Jake was quiet. He's been quiet. I can't even pretend to know what he's thinking about now and I hate that. It messes me up.

"Fadley! Gardner! In the name of our Lord Jesus Christ, *when* are you going to start painting that thing?"

I jump. Norton got us from behind. I turn and give him my sweetest smile, but he only raises one very unimpressed eyebrow at me. I think my haircut has actually compromised the manipulative properties of my face.

"You of all people should know real art can't be rushed, Mr. Norton," I say.

"If *that* is real art, Fadley," Norton says, nodding at our paper, "then please direct me to that ravine so I can throw myself into it."

Jake stares determinedly at our landscape. It's not *that* bad.

"Art is subjective," I remind Norton.

"That it is, Fadley. Nevertheless, I suggest you get a move on. Your landscapes are due at the end of this week."

The room explodes. This is news to everyone. Jake's mouth drops open and several students make a mad scurry to the supply cabinet to get more paint. I ignore the voice in my head telling me to vomit. I want to graduate. I want to graduate. I want to graduate. Or else I'll be stuck here forever.

"Oh my!" Norton looks around the room in mock surprise and genuine delight. Old bastard. "Did I forget to tell all of you?"

"Okay, that's it," Jake says. "We need a plan and we need it now."

"I can't think," I say. I really can't. What if this is it? What if this is the stupid thing that keeps me from graduating? Unity, disparity. Unity. My fingers start tingling. I press my hands flat on the desk. Don't think about it.

"Come on, Parker," Jake says desperately. "Give me something, anything."

"Jake, shut up. I can't—"

"Why am I not surprised?" he snaps.

He wanders to the back for the paint, returning with five or six different colors, but by the time the period ends, neither of us has attempted a start.

I zombie-walk to the gym, completely forgetting about the chapel, and when I get there the cheerleaders are preparing to practice and Evan is preparing to play basketball and everyone sees me come in, so I can't leave.

Chris walks over.

"How did you get here?"

"I walked," I murmur, staring past him. I can't lose sight. I have to fix it.

"Come on; let's get you back inside. You can crash in my room."

"No—" I blink and *Jessie and the guy she's with have gone. Disappeared. They were by the pool and now they're not and I haven't fixed it. I turn to Chris. "Where did they—where did they go?"*

"Where did who go?"

"They—" And then this song starts up, really loud. I can't think. If I can't think, I can't find Jessie; I can't fix it. I have to find Jessie. "Chris, this music makes me feel like, it's like—"

He laughs.

"Okay, when you start talking about how the music makes you feel, maybe it's time for you to go to bed. Come on, Parker."

He tries to force me toward the house, but I jerk away.

"You're not listening to me! Just listen to me—"

"Okay, just—it's okay." But he's patronizing me. He has this stupid patronizing, condescending voice on and he thinks I'm too drunk to hear it. "Where are—"

And that's when she reappears, that strange guy beside her. No. A different guy. I relax. They start dancing and she stands on her tiptoes and kisses him, this new guy, and my stomach turns because I did this.

Evan removes himself from the basketball game before it really starts. He jogs across the gym, to the bleachers where I'm sitting, and the vise around my heart gets tighter and tighter, but I think I'll be okay as long as I focus solely on breathing. But if he starts talking to me I'm worried I won't be able to talk back and breathe at the same time.

"Hi, Parker," he says, sitting beside me. "I've been hoping to talk to you."

Inhale. "Oh?" Exhale.

Okay, maybe I can do this after all.

"Yeah. We haven't really talked. So, I mean . . ." He shrugs self-consciously. "Like, how are you? How've you been?"

Inhale. "You're missing the basketball game." Exhale.

"Not really. I'm so out of shape, passing the ball takes up most of my energy. Two minutes in and I'm on my third wind." He cracks a smile. I edge away, but he doesn't notice. "Not much changes at St. Peter's, huh? I mean it's like I never left."

"I wouldn't say that."

"Oh." That doesn't slip past him. "Okay."

"Yeah."

Oh, right—inhale. Exhale. I clench my hands into fists and glance down the court. Chris and Jake are involved in the game, but every so often one of them looks my way.

Call Evan back. Call him back and get him away from me.

"Man, I was hoping it wouldn't be like this," he says. "I wanted to talk to you."

I close my eyes.

"I have nothing to say to you, Evan."

"Hey, Parker!"

I open my eyes. Becky's staring at me expectantly, arms crossed. I can't even begin to imagine what she could possibly want with me.

"What?"

"Would you come down here and stand in place for Ellie? She's sick and I want to see the formation from the front without a big gaping hole in it. You don't have to do anything, just stand there."

"Sure."

I jump up and jog over to the squad. The girls are already in formation. I take a quick look back and Evan's where I left him, staring at me. I don't like that.

"Where do you want me?" I ask Becky.

"Over there, between Sarah and Hannah," she says, pointing. "Are you okay?"

The girls stare at us, awaiting instruction. Robots.

"Why?"

"You look weird." She smiles. "And *not* just because of the hair."

I wipe my palms on my skirt. Block it out. He's not there.

"As former captain, I'm trying to get over my disgust that you can't use your imagination to pretend Ellie's in her usual spot," I say. A couple girls gasp. "I did that for all of those practices *you* managed not to show up for."

Becky scowls. "Are you going to help me or not?"

"Oh, I'm not helping you, Becky. I'm here for my own amusement."

With that, I flounce into Ellie's spot, and Becky climbs a little way up the bleachers to inspect us.

"Okay, it's good," she shouts. "Parker, stay there. The rest of you show me what victory looks like!"

The girls stretch their arms into the *V*. Evan's still looking at me. I want him to stop. They move onto the *I*. I glance down the court again.

Come on, Chris. Call Evan back.

Make him stop.

I pull at my collar. It's hot in this gym; it's—*T. O.* I realize I'm not breathing again. I'm not breathing and it's hot. The scene turns to mush. I try to blink it back into focus. The girls are moving in slow motion but not really, but they *are* standing too close and if Evan doesn't stop staring at me I'll—

"Somebody get Henley or something."

I don't want to open my eyes.

"Just wait. Parker? Can you hear me? Parker?"

I am not going to open my eyes. I'm going to lie on the court until I die, and I hope that happens soon, because I want to die.

"Okay, someone get Henley."

After a minute, I open my eyes. Chris notices first.

"Hey," he says.

Jake glances at him. Then me. He exhales, relieved.

"You're okay."

If he says so, it must be true. I stare at everyone staring at me. The entire stupid cheerleading squad and all of the brainless hard-core jocks. This is great.

I will the floor to open up and eat me alive.

"Hey, let's give her some space. Get back to the game, guys," Chris says. Thank God for him, just this once. "And cheerleading. Get back to that, too." No one moves. "Okay, fuck off, basically, is what I'm saying. Fuck off!"

Everyone mumbles in assent and scatters back to opposite sides of the court. That's what it's like to be popular. Becky lingers a minute before remembering she's captain and Jake helps me into sitting position and I try to think of something clever and smart-ass to say, but I can't and it freaks me out.

Chris crouches down and hands me his water bottle.

"Drink that." He looks so concerned. "You'll feel better."

I take a small sip and hand the bottle back. Maybe the first words out of my mouth don't have to be totally smart-ass. Just normal.

But I have nothing.

And that's when I notice Evan's not around. Gone. And then I wonder if he was ever here at all and my hands start shaking because seriously, what if he wasn't and I'm losing it? I try to hide my hands, but Jake sees and he gives me this look and I *still* can't think of anything to say and it's quiet.

And then Henley comes in and Evan is with her. Oh.

"What happened here?"

I wish for once she'd look surprised to see me. I move to get up, but Jake puts a hand on my shoulder, stopping me, while Chris explains the situation to the best of his limited vocabulary. I meet Evan's eyes and I guess I'm sending out the right *go away* vibes, because he skulks off to play basketball with the rest of the guys.

When Chris is finished, Henley regards me carefully. Even she has more couth than to ask whether or not I've been drinking or whatever in front of everyone. But it should be painfully obvious I haven't, because I don't look happy.

"Nurse's office," she says. "Can you walk, Fadley?"

I get to my feet with Jake's unneeded assistance.

"I want to go home," I say.

Except my voice cracks and just like that I'm totally overwhelmed by how stupid this feels and the edges of my mouth start pulling themselves down like they always do when I'm about to cry and then I realize *I'm about to cry*. I cover my eyes. *Don't cry.*

Don't cry.

"Fadley?"

"I—" If I don't lower my hands, they'll think I'm crying anyway, and I can't let them think that so I drop my hands to my sides. "I don't want to go to the nurse's office. I don't feel well. I want to go home."

Jake and Chris stare at me funny. Maybe they think it's a crock.

I mean, even Henley doesn't really seem convinced, but she never does.

But Bailey believes me. I spend the evening sitting in a chair by my window and he guards me diligently, ready to ward off any intruders that dare disturb me. He actually growls a little the first time my bedroom door opens, but he wags his tail when he sees it's Mom. It's Mom, even though I told her to leave me alone because I know I make her feel the worst when I make her feel useless.

She tugs at a strand of my hair and sighs.

"At least let me even out the edges, Parker."

I rub my wrist. I wish it was there. The bracelet.

"If I do, will you let me stay home from school for the next two days?"

She's quiet for a long time, debating it.

"Fine," she finally says. "I'll get the scissors. Meet me in the kitchen."

Bailey follows me downstairs, where Mom's set up barbershop—a chair atop scattered newspapers in the middle of the room. She stands behind it, waiting, scissors in one hand. I sit.

"I worry about you, Parker," she says, gently pushing my head forward. I want to tell her to join the club and then I want to tell her how boring that makes her and to not be so tedious. But I don't. Snip, snip, snip. "You used to talk to me."

But I never *said* anything.

"You were so . . ."

Perfect. She never finishes, but I know if she had, that's what she would've said. *Perfect. You were so.*

When she's finished evening out my hack job, my hair that used to fall past my shoulders now stops at my chin. And it looks horrible.

Which is good, I guess.

eighteen

"Hey, Parker?"

I slam my locker shut. Evan.

He's incredibly in-my-face for a guy who knows I want nothing to do with him, but at least I'm more capable of handling myself now. During my two-day vacation I did a little cognitive behavior therapy and taught myself this anxiety transference trick, where I effectively turn the feeling that my heart wants to claw its way out of my chest into sheer annoyance and total anger every time I see him.

Which means my hands might still shake, but the difference is that it's not going to end in total nervous collapse.

Here's hoping it works.

"What." It's not a question; it's a statement. And I spit it at him.

He cringes.

"I'm sorry, I know you don't want to . . ." He shifts and just blurts it out: "Look, do you remember that party last year, I mean, like, at all?"

"Why?"

"Because—" He takes one look at my face and shakes his head. "You know what? Never mind. Chris said you didn't."

"Well, don't take him at his word or anything; he's only your best friend." My voice oozes sarcasm. In our old lives, Evan and I didn't like each other very much. This feels like slipping on a pair of comfortable old shoes. "Thanks for wasting my time."

"I had to ask," he says, but he doesn't go.

"I barely remember it," I lie; if anything, I remember it too well. Then I pretend to spot someone over his shoulder. "Oh, hi, Jenny! Have you welcomed Evan back yet?"

He turns white and whirls around. Jenny's not there, of course, and he should know that, but when he faces me, furious patches of red decorate his pale face.

"If anything, you're an even bigger bitch than you used to be," he mutters. He storms off, not knowing how reaffirming it is to hear that. I feel steadier on my feet than I have in days. Still got it.

I put on a radiant smile for art and sit next to Jake.

"So, I think I've finally got an idea for our project," I say without adding *you know, the one that's due tomorrow?* "We might have to put in some time after school, but I didn't think you'd mind very much."

"Forget it," Jake says. "I already handed it in."

"Okay, so what we do is—" I stop and process. "What?"

"While you were gone, I just did it. I took it home and I did it. Handed it in yesterday. You don't have to worry about it."

"Oh."

"Norton seemed to like it. So we've got the period to draw whatever we want."

I nod slowly. "Okay."

I get us paper from the supply closet and my mind is going a thousand thoughts a second but never settles on one. I used to be good at improvising.

I set the paper in front of him.

"Why would you do that?" I ask.

"I figured you had enough to deal with."

"You mean you felt sorry for me."

"Did I say that?" He grabs a pencil and starts doodling. "I don't feel sorry for you, but do you really think you could've gotten yourself together enough to help me get our project finished? But be honest when you answer."

"That's not fair."

"You're the one who disappeared for two days."

I snap my fingers.

"You know, you were acting strange on Monday," I finally say. "Like, weird. I *knew* I shouldn't have gone to the dance with you—"

"I was acting like how *you* wanted me to act," he points out calmly.

"Yeah, and then some."

"What's it to you?"

"It's—" Goddammit. I snap my fingers again. "Are you trying to back me into a corner so I'll date you or something? Because here's a little advice for you: girls don't like being emotionally blackmailed."

"What am I blackmailing you with? I don't have anything you want."

"I—"

"Look, I made this decision after the dance," he says. "I don't want to screw around since you've made it pretty clear you're not interested in actually starting anything. You should be happy. It works out for you better this way."

"I like it the other way," I say stupidly.

"Too bad."

"You can't just *not* like me. Feelings don't go away like that.

Ask Chris. He's still totally in love with me and it's been months and months."

But it occurs to me I don't know if that's true anymore.

"I'll get over it," Jake says, his eyes meeting mine.

"Fine, fine, fine," I say quickly, still snapping. I don't know why I care, but I don't like him getting to decide this. It's mine to decide. "If that's the way you want it, let's go out. Let's go out tonight. I'll take you out. How about that?"

He falters. I can tell.

"I can't. I'll be at Chris's tonight."

"How about after? Or are you staying the night?"

"I'm staying. We're going to Whitney tomorrow, to this old car exhibit."

"Is Evan going to be there?"

"Not that I'm aware of."

"Why?"

He shrugs. "Ask him yourself."

I corner Chris on his way to his last class.

"Aren't you still best friends with Evan?"

He blinks. "I like your hair. I'm getting used to it."

"How come you didn't invite Evan to that stupid old car exhibit?"

"Because Evan's not into stupid old cars?"

"Evan wasn't into a ton of stuff you liked and you made him do it anyway. So are you still best friends with him or what?"

"Why?"

"I have to know."

He glances at his wristwatch.

"I don't have time for the 'things change' speech, Parker."

"So give me the CliffNotes version."

"Okay. You ready?" he asks. I nod. "Things change."

"*Chris.*"

He makes an exasperated noise.

"He just got back and there happens to be this event in Whitney that I think I'd probably have a better time at if I took Jake along. Over Evan. Satisfied?"

I shake my head. "No."

"Why?"

"I don't know." Everything feels wrong. I start snapping my fingers again. "But what about me? How do you feel about me? You're still hung up on me, aren't you?"

"Parker—"

"This is your fault," I say. "You made me go to the dance."

His mouth drops open.

I go to the girls' washroom and pace because my brain is telling me to do something and this is it. Pace. This is *so* annoying; last week I had the whole school and everyone in it and now things are different and I hate it. The door opens, but I pace in spite of it. Anyway, it's Becky, so it doesn't matter.

"Oh," she says when she sees me. She walks over to the sink, pencil case in hand because that's where she keeps her makeup. "Hi."

I watch, still pacing, as she takes out her lipstick and gets to work.

"What do you and Chris talk about?"

The lipstick hovers above her lower lip. She stares at me in the mirror.

"None of your business?"

"Do you talk about, like, the deep stuff? Important stuff? Or just basketball and cheerleading? Or is it a sex thing and you don't talk at all?"

She does her lips and caps her lipstick before she even dignifies that with an answer, which drives me crazy.

"What did you and Chris talk about?" she asks.

"Everything," I say quickly. "Our conversations were deep and profound."

"Would you quit pacing?"

I can't stop. I want to tell her that, but I don't.

And I wouldn't stop anyway, now that I know she wants me to.

"Do you talk about Evan and stuff?"

"And stuff," she repeats faintly, smiling a little. "And stuff? Yeah, we talk about Evan 'and stuff.'"

"Do you talk about me?"

She crosses her arms. "What is *wrong* with you, Parker?"

"Is Chris over me? I mean—" I stop pacing. "Is he?"

"Your name doesn't come up so much anymore."

I snap my fingers. Both of them. Again and again.

"Just like that?"

"Just like that."

"I don't believe you."

I leave the washroom as the bell rings, Becky calling after me.

I've got my usual meeting with Grey, and for once in my life I'm glad. Finally, someone I can predict. I enter her office, sit down, and we say nothing and I feel a little better. At least there's still one person in this school who can be counted on.

After the first fifteen minutes of quiet, she starts flipping through a magazine.

I blink.

I'm on the lawn, by the bushes where I threw up. I blink again and I'm next to Chris. I blink again and Jessie's dancing, making out with a new mystery guy, different from the last one. Where do they all come from? I blink again and Evan's there, screaming at both of them. I blink again and someone's pulling Chris away because something's broken, a lamp or a vase.

I blink again and I'm alone, in front of the drinks

table set out on the lawn. I'm here because I'm thirsty. My hands drift over the booze and go straight for the bowl of punch for the designated driver. I fill up a cup with shaking hands and drink it, then another.

It's passion fruit or strawberry Hawaiian something and it tastes good.

Then, a voice behind me:

"Someone spiked that, like, an hour ago."

I drop the cup and moan.

"Oh, God."

Becky laughs. "Good one."

I shuffle over to a soft patch of grass and sit down. Someone will probably have to peel my alcohol-bloated corpse off the lawn come morning.

"Chris wants me to get you inside," Becky says, grabbing my arms and pulling. She stumbles forward and giggles, her face in my face, beer on her breath. "Come on."

"Where's Jessie?"

"Somewhere. I was just talking to her," she says brightly, pulling on my arm again. She gives up and sits beside me. "She and Evan are so over, by the way. Well done, Parker. I should console him."

"You would."

Then I remember it's my mission to fix what I did, because it's wrong and I don't do things that are wrong. The goal swims in front of my mind and starts to drift away, but I try really hard to hold on to it. And then I close my eyes.

Maybe after I sleep.

"Did you see them fighting by the pool? So over," she says again, giggling. My head snaps up. "Big surprise. Me and Evan, we'd make a much better match."

"Parasite," I say. I blink several times, trying to snap myself out of this fuzzy place. "It's never going to happen."

"It will. We have tons in common." Tipsy Becky is a thousand times more annoying than sober Becky, and that's saying something. "So when are you going to relinquish captaining duties to me, anyway?"

"Fuck off and die first and then we'll talk," I mumble, feeling my head go forward. It wants to sleep. No. I jerk upright. It doesn't really help.

"I'll be captain in a week." Her voice is hard, too hard, and it dawns on me through the murk that she's only pretending to be drunk, which is one of her favorite party tricks because she's under this bizarre delusion it's cute. "You'll finally snap or the rest of the girls will vote you off the squad. Whichever comes first."

"Brave to say so in front of me." I struggle to push myself up from the ground, but it's just not happening. "I could ruin your life."

"You won't remember any of this," she says.

"What makes you think you deserve to be captain?"

"I'm nicer than you, for starters." She goes quiet for so long I think that's it, I can pass out, but no, she starts talking again. "I'm nice to everyone and no one gives a damn. You tear people down and act like you're doing them a favor and they act like you're Jesus because they're stupid enough to believe it. At least they're starting to catch on now. Not even being Chris's girlfriend is helping you. And I'm so looking forward to making everyone realize how much better they could've had it with me."

"That's really pathetic." I have to force every word through my teeth. "And I'll remember this, Becky."

She snorts.

"Where's Jessie?" I use Becky's shoulder to get into standing position. The world tilts. For a second, I think I'll be sick, but I'm not and I'm standing and it's a miracle. "Becky, where is she?"

"I talked to her for a minute, after she and Evan fought. She was crying her eyes out. She said she was going to run away. Drama Queen." Becky looks up at me and smiles. "Nice going, Parker."

"Where did she go?"

Becky points in the direction of the woods.

nineteen

They could be talking about me, like, right now.

Chris and Jake.

I hate that.

So after I choke down dinner I decide to take Bailey for a walk. I slip on my shoes, call him from the living room and hook him up to the leash. He figures out what's going on and squirms and slobbers all over me.

"I thought dogs were supposed to mellow with age," I tell him. He flicks his tongue at my face and I back away just in time. "Jesus, Bailey."

"Parker, don't talk like that in the house," Mom says. "It's disrespectful."

Jesus, Jesus, Jesus.

"I'll see you guys later."

"Have a nice walk, sweetheart." Dad.

"Be home by nine." Mom. I don't say anything. "I mean it, Parker."

"Yeah, sure," I say, and then, for good measure: "Whatever."

So I leave and we walk, and it's an okay walk. I steer Bailey onto Chris's street without realizing it. Actually, that's a lie. I know what I'm doing.

I know what I'm doing and it's stupid.

But Bailey pulls me forward at a happy trot, his tongue always and forever hanging out of his mouth. The closer we get to Chris's house, the more uneasy I feel, but maybe I'd feel better to pass it once and then go home.

So that's what I'll do.

We're practically there when this string of cars go by, one after the other, and I feel criminal, caught. It makes me want to turn back, but I can't because the thought is there, that I should pass the house. So I have to.

This is *so* stupid.

And then this explosion of sound fills the street, like a small bomb going off—an engine backfiring—and Bailey yelps and tears loose because I'm not holding the leash tightly enough. He runs into the road and before I can call him back or go after him, there are all these other sounds, smaller sounds, this dull thud, squealing tires.

And then silence.

Just like that.

He lies in the middle of the street, his legs splayed out before him the way they are when he sleeps on the living-room floor. I go to him, kneel down in front him. He stares up at me, pitiful but alive. But what kind of—

What kind of asshole *hits a dog and drives away?*

Bailey shudders.

"Bailey. Bailey—Bailey . . ."

I spew his name. I say it a thousand times in three seconds. I rest my hand on his stomach and it comes back red and he makes a noise, this awful whimper.

"Stop that," I snap. "You're fine. We'll just get you off the—"

I wrap my arms around him so I can drag him off the road, but I don't have the strength to lift him and my shirt gets red. I have to let him go.

I wasn't holding the leash tightly enough.

"Don't," I tell him. "You're fine. I'll get someone. I'll—"

I stand. I don't have a lot of time. I need—

Chris. Chris can fix this; he's rich.

I run to his house and pound on the door and ring the bell at the same time and it seems like hours before the door actually opens and there he is.

Chris.

"What the fuck—" He stops, his eyes traveling from my face to my hands to my shirt. The parts of me that are red. "Parker, what happened?"

"My dog got hit by a car. I don't know what to do."

He stares at me uncomprehendingly and then Jake appears behind him and gives me this surprised look and Bailey is dying.

"What's going on?" Jake asks.

I don't have time for this. I'm wasting time. I run back down the driveway and they both follow after me, calling my name.

But they quiet when Bailey comes into view.

"Oh God," Chris mutters.

My pulse is in my ears, loud and insistent.

When we get to Bailey, he's still.

"I'm so sorry, Parker," Jake says.

For a second, I think my heart is going to explode.

But then the feeling goes away.

"This engine backfired or something; it really scared him." I stare at Bailey's body. It doesn't even look real. "I wasn't holding the leash tightly enough."

"Did you see who did it?" Jake asks.

"No—I thought there'd be time to do something for him,"

I say stupidly. I wish his eyes would close. Bailey's. "Sorry for dragging you out. . . ."

"It's okay," Chris says.

"No, it's not. I should really go."

I stand and start heading down the street without looking back at either of them. I want to get far away from Bailey's body. Take a shower. Get his blood off of me. I pull at my shirt. Off of me.

"Parker, where are you going?"

I stop and turn. I hear the question, but . . .

"Your house is that way." Chris points in the opposite direction.

"I'll get there eventually."

"Why don't you come inside and I'll make tea or something."

"No thanks."

"I know you," he says. "You won't go home."

"I *can't* go home."

"You can stay at my place tonight."

No.

"You have that car show."

"Forget it," Jake says.

Chris holds out his hand.

"Come on."

"I wasn't holding the leash tightly enough."

I don't know why I say it again. They look at me funny. And then Chris takes me by the elbow and the three of us walk up to his house.

I can't feel my feet.

I can't feel my feet and the night has all caught up with me, but I soldier on. The farther I get from the house, the louder the music sounds. A heavy bass line and an earsplitting drumbeat winds its way into the woods from Chris's open bedroom window. And then there's splashing sounds coming from the pool and everyone's laughing and talking and shrieking and having a good time.

Because Chris's parties are the best except when they're not.

Twenty-five steps into the woods, I think about lying down or turning back. I can't feel my feet, I can't feel my legs, anything, and my head is barely attached to my neck, but I've got to fix this because I'm supposed to be better than this and what if everyone finds out I'm not.

A few more steps. I hear something and I stop.

"Go to the guest room, take a shower and grab a nightshirt. You know where everything is," Chris says, closing the door behind us. "Come down and we'll have . . . tea."

"Tea," I repeat faintly. "Do you even know how to make tea?"

"It can't be that hard," he says, heading for the kitchen.

I go upstairs. I sit on the bed in the guest room. I don't even feel like showering anymore. I just want to sit here with Bailey's blood on me while he's splayed out on the middle of the road.

He can't stay there forever.

After a while, I tiptoe down the hall to Chris's parents' bedroom, steal into their bathroom and turn on the light. I stare at myself in the mirrored cabinet. I look really bad. I open the cabinet and stare at the prescription bottles inside.

Chris's mom was a desperate housewife before it was cool.

I grab the bottle of pills that make you happy and let you go to sleep, open it up and empty them beside the sink. I start counting them out, and when I've done that I arrange them in neat rows of six.

I can make out two shapes in the darkness, on the

ground. On a bed of pine needles. My heart sinks. I inch forward quietly and hold my breath. If she's fucked him, this is—this is harder to fix. Jessie's fucking him.

"What are you doing?"

My hand jerks into the rows of pills and some of them scatter into the sink. I scramble to prevent as many of them from going down the drain as I can, but it's futile, they all go, and anyway, it doesn't matter.

I start putting what's left of them back.

"Why don't you tell me what you think I'm doing?" I ask.

"I don't even want to say it."

I rub my hands on my shirt.

"I just wanted one to sleep. Your mom has the good stuff."

"A whole bottle is hardly one."

"I wanted to pick the right one."

"Oh, duh. I should have known."

"I—" I force myself to look Chris in the eyes. "I have to take that shower."

"Fine. But if it takes longer than ten minutes I'm coming back up to get you."

I take the shower, but I make sure it's a long one just to see if he'll come in. He doesn't, like I knew he wouldn't. Because the air is different now. I'm far away from the pills and they're far away from me, but Bailey's still out on the road, dead, not far away at all, and he can't stay there forever.

I come out of the bathroom and change into one of the nightshirts they leave for the guests and wrap myself up in one of the guest housecoats.

And then I put on my best face and head downstairs.

"—But we have to move him," Jake's saying. "Should we get Parker?"

"She's upset. We could do it for her," Chris says. Pause.

"I don't know. Maybe she wants to be there for it. Maybe we should get her."

Silence.

"Well, which is it?"

"I don't know," Chris says again. "I hate this."

It gets heavy quiet. I sneak out the back door, putting as much distance as possible between me and the house. I thought I knew why I was coming out here, but now, between the road and woods, I'm not so sure.

I head for the woods.

It's extremely quiet. No matter how close I get to all the trees, even memories of sound are hushed by the death out on the street.

And then I'm in the woods. In them. Just far enough in.

I get down on my hands and knees and start brushing pine needles aside. Maybe the bracelet will show up again. Maybe I'm supposed to lose it every so often and then I'm supposed to find it again and Bailey was supposed to die because it's here for me, like it was before. And then I can wear it around my wrist, for both of them—

Bailey.

I can't do this. What am I doing?

I leave the woods and make my way to the road, to do what I should've done in the first place. He's still there, all broken and stiff, and I think I hate him for it. I kneel in front of his body and rest my hand on his chest, hoping for a heartbeat even though I know there won't be one.

Or maybe . . .

I rest my head against his chest and listen. His fur is scratchy and unpleasant against my skin, not soft like it was, the blood on it caked and flaking.

I close my eyes and I really listen.

Come on, Bailey, you stupid dog.

Come on.

Please.

"Parker?"

It's Jake.

"My dog's dead," I say. He kneels beside me, but he doesn't say anything, so I keep talking. "I knew this would happen."

"You couldn't have predicted that car."

"Yeah, I could have," I say. "Because that's what I do to people. And now dogs. I just fuck them up. And it's always spectacular how I do it, too. But—maybe not before. I wouldn't have predicted it *before*. But now I can."

He stares at me, concerned. I feel off my head.

"What do you mean?" he asks.

"Before I thought I was above letting these kinds of things happen, but now I know that's not the truth. Now it's just a matter of time before they do. And I knew if Bailey—" I gaze at my dog's prone form. He was my dog. "I knew it would end like this. And here we are."

"Here we are."

"It shouldn't upset me that you guys are done with me," I say. "Because that's what I want."

"Really," Jake says. "That's what you want?"

"Yeah. I just forget it sometimes, I guess. I don't know."

"You don't know?"

"You're echoing everything I say." I meet his eyes and I can't believe how it wasn't that long ago he was just this new kid and I kind of scared him and somewhere along the way I got lazy and let him get close, so I guess that means he'll get hit by a car or something, too. "I like certain things a certain way or it's not right. But I've been forgetting."

"I'm sorry," he says.

"But he was a good dog," I say after a minute, running my hand over Bailey's head, the way he liked it when he was alive. Alive. I swallow. "And I have to move him. I can't leave him here."

"Parker, I can . . ." He hesitates. "Do you need help?"

My answer gets stuck in my throat and stays there, never passing my lips.

It doesn't matter.

Together, we move Bailey off the road.

twenty

Mom decides we should bury Bailey under the maple tree in the backyard. She asked me what I thought about it and I said I didn't care, but she just kept at it and kept at it and I just wanted her to shut up, so in the end I had to remind her about the time I told her I couldn't have cared less if Bailey died, and it worked. She shut up.

And she hasn't really spoken to me since.

"It felt like we had him longer." Mom wipes her eyes. Dad nods and wraps an arm around her. "We should have had him longer."

That's a dig at me.

"I guess it was just his time," Dad says after a while.

"Lucky him," I say.

It just slips out.

"What did you say?" Dad's voice is sharp. He gives me this look. I shrug and march away from the whole scene, but he keeps talking. "Parker, get back here and tell me what you said—Parker!"

"What did she say?" Mom asks.

And of course they can't just leave it at that. On Monday, on my way to catch the school bus, my little slip-of-the-tongue turns into this:

"Make sure you come straight home after school."

I pause at the door.

"Why?"

"Because your mother and I need to talk with you."

Think quick, Parker.

"I can't."

Dad lowers the paper and looks at me, like, I don't know.

"Why?"

"I promised Becky I'd give her some tips about these new cheerleading routines she's planned. She's not feeling so confident about them. And then I was going to . . ." I fumble for the words. "I was going to stay the night. I forgot to ask. Sorry."

He frowns and thinks about it. Doesn't even notice I don't have an overnight bag or anything, but doesn't want to believe that after all this I would still lie. It's sad.

"Fine," he says, returning to the paper. "Tomorrow then."

"Death freaks me out," Jake says suddenly.

It's going to be one of those days.

"Thanks for sharing," I say. I'm filling my blank sheet of paper with circles and he's drawing a tree. Art is back to normal, as in no one really cares. "I don't know what I ever would have done had you not told me that about you."

He frowns.

"I don't like it. It always makes me take stock. And then I have to go through this process where I have to decide how important things are and if I'm doing enough about them. That freaks me out, too. Does that happen to you? . . . Did it happen to you?"

"Nope."

"So I called my mom."

I stop drawing and give him my full attention because if we're talking about this we're not talking about Bailey or me.

"What happened?"

He squints at his paper.

"She thought I was calling to beg to come back home. It didn't go so well when she found out I wasn't."

"That sucks."

"Yeah."

"So what are you going to do about it?"

"What can I do about it?" He shrugs. "She's decided; I've decided. I called her and she shut me out."

"Does it make you feel worse or better?"

He thinks about it for a second.

"I thought I'd be happy for the closure. But it's worse, actually. I feel guilty."

"So what happens next?"

He shrugs again.

"I keep going from here?"

We reach for the white gummy eraser sitting between us at the same time. His hand brushes over mine and then lingers there and I freeze.

"Your hand is on my hand," I say in this completely stupid voice.

And then Chris struts over under Norton's disapproving gaze, but since the sun is shining and it's nice out he's feeling lenient enough not to shout Chris back to his seat.

"Hey, Jake. Rain check tonight."

"What?" Jake turns around. "What the fuck?"

"Sorry," Chris says, glancing at me and looking away. "It's just that Becky's got romantic-type plans."

I roll my eyes. Becky's idea of "romantic" is no underwear.

"So?" Jake asks.

"So," Chris says slowly, leaning forward, "I can either fuck Becky or dick around with you. What do you think I'm going to choose?"

"Oh, fuck off," Jake mutters. "Asshole."

Chris punches him in the arm.

"Thanks, man. I knew you'd understand."

"You've got until I count to three to get back to your seat, Ellory," Norton says lazily from the front of the room. "One . . . two . . ."

Chris scurries away.

"Plans tonight?" I ask.

"Not anymore," Jake grumbles. "I'm on a two-day vacation from my parents. It was going to be a guys' night in, blow off school tomorrow. We've been planning it forever."

"Sounds pretty hot."

"I was hoping," he says, grinning. "I mean, look at him. He's so built."

"You're preaching to the choir, Jake." We draw in silence for a little bit and I'm thinking, thinking, thinking. I know how to take advantage of every situation and I've got nowhere to sleep tonight. "If you ask me over right now, there's a ninety percent chance I'll say yes."

Jake stops drawing, but he doesn't look at me.

"Are you serious?"

"Eighty. It's eighty percent now." Pause. "Seventy . . ."

"Come over?"

I stare at all the circles I've drawn.

"Yeah."

On the bus ride there's only quiet between us. Jake leads me off at his stop and we walk up Trudeau Road, to his house near the end of it. I recognize the place. It's a small bungalow with a neat front lawn and a cute little garden along the path to the front door. The shutters are faded pink. It's the kind of house that might as well have a sign that says GOOD PEOPLE LIVE HERE mounted in front of it.

"How did you finish our art project anyway?" I ask while Jake unlocks the front door. "What did you do in the end?"

"Oh," he says, pausing. "I painted half of it and let the other half stay unfinished. I don't think even Norton knew what he was talking about when he said all that bullshit about unity and disparity. He *was* just fucking with us. But he enjoyed the picture. Said the right side reminded him of you."

I'm not expecting that.

"Why?"

"It was the unfinished side. He was totally on to us."

I smile. "Seriously?"

"Yeah." He opens the door and steps aside. "But he still gave us an A, so it's all good."

The front door opens into the kitchen, which is a small, neat little room with a tiny breakfast nook that must serve as the lunch and dinner table as well.

"Nice place," I say automatically, because that's what you do.

"Thanks," Jake says. He sets his book bag on the floor, so I do the same. He makes a beeline for the fridge, totally relaxed. "Are you thirsty? Hungry?"

"Thirsty."

"Water, Coke, OJ? . . . Heineken?"

"Water, thanks."

He hands me a bottle, takes one for himself and leans against the kitchen counter, staring at me. He gets the upper hand because it's his house. I should've thought of that before I wrangled an invitation out of him. I twist the cap off my water and sip.

"Sure you're not hungry?" he asks after a minute.

This is weird.

"I'm sure."

"Well, I'm starving and I have to do something about it." He heads back to the fridge, rifles through it, and pretty soon he's got all the ingredients needed to make a sandwich massive enough to feed ten men or one teenage boy. "Hey, First Friday Mass is this Friday."

I groan. "Don't remind me."

"Yeah, tell me about it. What a waste of time." He looks at me. "Is that blasphemous? I don't know how you crazy Catholics operate."

"It's probably blasphemous."

He goes back to the fridge, retrieves an apple and tosses it to me.

"I never see you eat lunch," he says. "Eating is good for you."

I sit at the table and roll the apple along the varnished wood surface.

"You go to church a lot?" he asks, throwing everything imaginable between two thin slices of bread. For the first time since we got here, he sounds awkward. I don't want things to be awkward when we have the whole evening stretched out in front of us.

"Not outside of school, no."

It goes quiet, which makes everything else get loud. Jake finishes making his sandwich and the sound of his chewing is amplified by our silence, weirdly punctuating the moment. I stop rolling the apple and take a bite. It's so sweet, I almost gag.

"I miss my mom, though," Jake says randomly. "Before my dad fucked around on her she wasn't as bitter and crazy as she is now."

"Gee, who would've thought," I say.

He laughs.

"She really thought I was going to stay with her. Like, she

really—" He breaks off and shakes his head. "Anyway, that's the worst thing I've done. Chose my dad."

"That must be a relief for you," I say, setting the apple on the table. "Imagine if you'd done something really, really bad."

He stares at me, bemused.

"What's that supposed to mean?"

"She's your mom. She'll forgive you. You'll forgive her."

"It could be years from now."

"So you lose a little time. You still get to fix it."

He sips his water.

"What's the worst thing you've ever done?"

"None of your business." I run my finger along the ragged edges of the apple where I bit it. "Nothing that can be fixed."

"It can't be that bad."

"You don't know that, though, do you?"

"Okay. . . ." He chews his thumbnail. "It can't be fixed, so let it go."

"I'll just do that."

He's forgotten his sandwich. He tilts his head back and closes his eyes and stays that way for a minute. Then he opens his eyes and stares at me.

"How do you get to be an eighteen-year-old who's done something so unimaginably horrible it can't be fixed? I mean, seriously?"

"Where's your bathroom?"

He blinks.

"Through the living room, down the hall," he says, pointing. "It's the second door on the right."

I wander through his living room, which is sort of quaint and cozy, and down the narrow strip of hall with doors that offshoot into bedrooms, closets and bathrooms. The room opposite the bathroom catches my attention. It's unmistakably Jake's room, from the clothes piled on the floor to the unmade bed. I check to see if he's watching me from the kitchen. He's not.

I cross the hall and enter his room.

You can tell a lot about a person from their personal space, go figure. The posters on the wall make Jake's homesickness more evident than he ever would. There are no declarations of love for a particular band or movie, only shots of buildings in a city by the sea. I move to the bulletin board hanging over his desk and study the photographs tacked to it. Jake is in every single photo, naturally, and he's always surrounded by people and he always looks happy. I lean forward and peer at a photo of him wedged between two people who I'm guessing are his parents, pre-divorce.

He looks a lot like his mom.

"My yearbooks are on the bookshelf, if you're curious. And, uh, that's my underwear drawer over there and of course there's my closet. Snoop away."

I try not to let on he's startled me.

"Nice room," I say.

"It does the job." He's right behind me, really close. "You never answered my question."

"Don't you ever get tired of asking me questions?"

"Have to fill the moment somehow," he says.

I turn. We're close. Like, I Could Kiss Him close. I skirt around him and sit on the bed. He sits beside me and clears his throat.

"I just wonder what you're punishing yourself for, that's all," he says.

"I . . ." I clench my right hand, my fingernails digging into my palm. "I did something really wrong and I knew it was really wrong while I was doing it and I did it anyway."

"It happens."

"Not to me."

My eyes hurt and my throat is tight. But I don't want to cry in front of Jake because there's nothing in it for me.

"Oh hey," Jake says, alarmed, when the first tear gets by me. "I'm sorry."

Goddammit.

"You should be."

If my life were a movie, this would be the scene where I start blubbering and tell Jake to stay away from me or he'll just end up hurt or dead and, I don't know, maybe we'd kiss and try it anyway. But as fast as the tears come, they stop.

"Was it when—" He clears his throat. "Was it when you tried to kill yourself?"

I don't say anything.

"I mean . . . what was that like?"

I snort. "Well, it was obviously a very happy period in my life."

"Why are you doing that?"

"Doing what?"

"Snapping your fingers."

I look down. Sure enough, I'm snapping. He reaches over and grabs my hand. Holds it. I try to act like it doesn't bother me.

"I shouldn't have asked," he says.

It's just getting more and more awkward. There are *hours* until tomorrow.

"I stole a few hundred dollars from Chris and I got the hell out of Corby," I say after a minute. "I've never talked about it like this before. "And I got a big bottle of booze and a big bottle of sleeping pills. And I downed both. And then I got found. And then I got my stomach pumped."

"How close were you?"

"I don't know."

Not close enough.

The phone rings from some other room. Jake clears his

throat and the moment is over. I wonder how people lived with each other before they could learn to count on these types of inconveniences.

"I should get that," he says.

He leaves the room and a minute later his voice wafts into the bedroom from the kitchen and I can't think of anything to do, so I start rifling through his nightstand. I wouldn't do it if I knew he'd have a problem with it. Or maybe I would. Cough drops, condoms, old movie stubs and loose change. By the time Jake gets back, my hands are folded in my lap. He stands in the doorway, a silhouette.

"Parker, why are you here?" he asks.

"Do you want me to go?"

"No, no. It's—" He steps into the room and sits back down beside me. "I was just wondering why you're here. I mean, I'm *glad* you're here, but—"

I kiss him then, not to shut him up, but because I want to and because no one says things like *I'm glad you're here* to me anymore, which is mostly my fault, and I don't know, I don't want to keep coming back to him because it's better if I don't.

So I should get this part over with.

Jake kisses back. His lips are soft. My fingertips drift over his cheeks and I want this and I'm so caught up in how nice he feels and how nice he smells and the way he's touching me, I can almost pretend it's okay that I want this.

It's okay to want this. Everything's . . .

His mouth moves from my lips to my neck. I close my eyes.

"I'm glad I'm here," I murmur.

"What?" His voice tickles my skin. He heard it. I know he did.

"Nothing," I say, and his lips are on mine again.

I don't remember lying down, but we're lying down.

His hand slides up my shirt. He hesitates and I like the way his fingers dance around my skin, unsure, before his hands are all over me and mine are all over him and I half expect to check out, but I'm really there for it. It's not like at the dance, angry and forced. It's terrible in its gentleness and he's just wasting it on me.

twenty-one

"Leaving?"

Jake sounds disappointed and I don't turn around because I don't want to see it on his face. I finish off my glass of orange juice and set it in the sink.

"I can't skip," I say. "The school will call my parents, my parents will find out I lied about where I was, there will be a freak-out of epic proportions from both parties and I won't be able to graduate. You know how it is."

"You could've woken me up," he says. "I don't have time to catch the bus now."

"You should enjoy your day off," I say. "You planned it."

I finally turn around. Jake stands there, rumpled and sleepy eyed, hair sticking up at all sides. He smiles at me, crosses the room and gives me a kiss on the cheek and then the mouth. I count until it's over. It doesn't last very long. I mean, I'm not moving my lips or anything, so Jake can tell something's wrong.

"What?" he asks, pulling away.

"Nothing."

He studies me.

"This isn't going to end well, is it?"

"Well, now that you mention it . . ."

But I can't think of what else to say. I want to be biting about this, but it's harder once you've had sex with a person. Twice.

"Just say it," he says.

"It doesn't change anything," I tell him. "What we did."

"Yeah, it does."

"Okay, it does. But not the way you want it to."

"Oh, come on, Parker," he scoffs.

"I don't want a . . ." I struggle with the words. "I don't want to be with you."

"Why?"

"Because. I don't want be with you," I repeat slowly, making sure to look him in the eyes. "Especially not now that I've been with you."

It's the best I can do. He swallows. He's probably not taking it the way I mean it, and the way I mean it is that last night, after the first time we did it and I let him hold me, I knew I could ruin him. And I know I'm ruining him now, but it's different.

It's less.

"Is that it?"

"Yeah, that's it."

"You'll miss the bus," he says.

He pads out of the room and I feel empty and kind of surprised that for once in my life things would go the way I want them to. Because this is what I want, isn't it.

On my walk to the bus stop, I pass a dog stretched out on a lawn. It stares at me sort of accusingly.

It looks exactly like Bailey.

twenty-two

I'm avoiding Jake and Chris, and Mom and Dad have decided to send me to a real live shrink. Like, they've set up an appointment and everything, even though I still do my homework and I haven't missed one goddamn day of school. I can't figure it out. It's not like I binged on crystal meth, went crazy and shaved my head.

I cut my hair and our dog died.

So I trail Evan through the halls because I want to know how he does it. I'm not fooled for a second, not even with the haircut. The guy's practically dying in plain sight and everyone leaves him alone. I want that.

It takes three days for him to realize he's being shadowed. It all comes to a spectacular end when he makes a rough left turn and a sudden stop in the middle of the hall and I crash into him and my history books scatter all over the floor. The jig is up.

"Why are you following me?" he asks, bending down to retrieve my books. I rip them out of his hands. "Why have you *been* following me?"

"I—"

Wish I had liquid courage. My heart thuds in my chest and I can't even do that neat thing where I make myself get angry instead of anxious.

He stares at me, wary and expectant.

"Why are you back?" I finally manage.

"Why do you care?"

The only thing I can think to do is shake my head at him, and he's not interested in letting me waste his time, so he turns and goes the other way and I've got more pride than to chase after him, so I head back the way I came and crash right into someone—second time today my history books go flying.

"Jesus."

Not Jesus. Jake. He bends down and grabs my books.

"Great, thanks," I mutter, avoiding his eyes. Figures *now* all that anxiety would turn straight to rage. "What were you doing, following me? Were you just waiting for the opportunity to—"

He holds out my books without a word.

I grab them, but he doesn't let go.

"Let go," I say, tugging at them. "Give them to me."

His grip on my books tightens. His knuckles go white. I grit my teeth and make myself look at him because that's what he wants.

"It's not going to work," I say.

He releases the books. I clutch them to my chest and let him be the one who moves on. He passes me, close. I can smell him and for a second I think I'm in his bedroom again and his hand is trailing my cheek, my neck. In his bedroom where he kisses me and I sort of forget everything that came before it and everything that will have to come after. In his bedroom where I enjoy every single clumsy kiss and it surprises me, how I feel about it. Him. By the time we finish, it's not that I'm—I mean, I don't know what I am, so we do it again and later I realize it wasn't that I was happy, it was that I wasn't heavy, that there were these brief moments where the thing I make sure I live with wasn't in every breath in and out. And that scares me because it's not supposed to be that easy. Because that's wrong. I'm supposed to be paying for this for the rest of my life.

Because that's right.

"I don't want to see this shrink," I announce. "I won't go."

Dinnertime. Dad's at one end of the table, Mom at the other. My declaration causes Mom to stop sipping her drink and Dad sets his fork down and rests his chin in his hands. Their eyes meet and they have a telepathic conversation about it.

I hear every word and I don't like what they're saying.

She's going to the shrink, right?

Of course she's going to the shrink.

We're good parents.

And then they both look at me like I'm—I don't like the way they look at me.

Dad sighs and picks up his fork again. "You have to see her."

"I see Grey. I see Grey once a week. That's enough."

"She says you're uncooperative," Mom says. "She says you never talk."

"I'm not seeing a shrink. I'm not. I don't—"

"Her name is Georgina Bellamy," Dad interrupts gently. "She's an excellent psychiatrist. She specializes in talking to teenagers who need help."

"I don't *need* help." They don't say anything. I push my plate away and cross my arms. "I'm not going. I'm not going to say it again."

"We should've done it sooner," Mom says to Dad, like I'm not even in the room. "The first time she got in trouble after—"

"I'll hate you for it," I say over her.

Dad turns to me. "If that's what it takes to get you back—"

"Oh, *please*. That's so pathetic. *This* is pathetic. Is this because of . . . is this because of what I—" Calm down, Parker; calm down. Calm. "Is this about Bailey? Because I didn't want him to die; I just said that—"

It gets really quiet. And then Mom speaks.

"You know, after we buried Bailey, I came in and I thought—I don't even *know* you anymore. I don't even know my own daughter. You're not the *same*, Parker." She starts to cry. "You're not the same."

"I'm going to bed," I say, standing. I have had enough.

But Dad stands, too. He stands between me and my only way out of the room.

"You should just give up," I tell him, but it comes out sounding like a plea and he looks so worried from behind his glasses I want to break something.

And then he makes his way over to me and wraps me up into this hug and I feel myself go rigid. I let my arms hang at my sides.

"Don't say that," he says. "Don't even think it."

This is unbelievable. They still have hope for me.

I have done something wrong if they still have hope.

twenty-three

I open my locker and stare at the bottle of Jack resting on the top shelf.

It feels like it's been there forever, and every time I retrieve my books I'm always a little surprised no one's noticed the attractive, almost demure square bottle full of pale amber liquid, half-hidden by the black label with boastful white lettering I've never read beyond the name. All I need to know is how hard it messes you up, and Jack Daniel's has a tendency to do that like nothing else. I was a vodka girl before, because it was easier to hide in school and didn't make me as sick, but Becky obviously wanted to see me fall on my face when she gave me that paper bag in the chapel.

And today I am going to make her a very happy girl.

I reach for the bottle at the same time a low rumble of sound travels through the hallway the way a ripple crosses a pond before hitting the bank and going back in on itself. I feel this disturbance—this strange interruption of peace—in the pit of my stomach when I think I hear a name.

I forget about the bottle and follow the undercurrent of

sound. The people I pass look at me like they know something, but how can they know anything? It's too early in the
morning to know anything. An invisible thread leads me down
the hall and around the corner where a group of people are
clustered around a sobbing girl.

I get closer. It's Becky. She's the one crying. She's con-
soled by Chris, who stands at her right side, and Jake is at
her left, looking out of place and awkward.

And I walk right past them, but Chris calls me back.

"Parker."

I backtrack slowly and face them, not just the three of
them, but three plus an audience, because I don't deserve
less. I clench my hands into fists, digging my nails in, and
wait for one or all of them to speak. Becky stops crying long
enough to raise her head from Chris's shoulder, and get ready
for it, Parker, because this is it.

*The party starts at eight, but I show up early so
Chris and I can have sex. We go to his bedroom.
He kisses me and I kiss him back and then, I don't
know, I kind of seize up.*

He flops back on his bed.

*"You should loosen the fuck up every once in a
while; the world wouldn't stop. No one would die."*

*We come downstairs looking like two people who've
spent the last thirty minutes having sex. Chris gets
to work on the tunes and I wind my way through the
house and spot Evan in the kitchen kissing Jenny
Morse. I clear my throat.*

*"Parker," Evan says nervously. He runs a hand
over his prickly black hair and holds out a bottle of
vodka and a shot glass. "Uh—shot?"*

*Jenny flees from the room. I take the bottle and
the glass and move to the kitchen counter, pour a
shot and knock it back. Then another.*

Evan watches. Hesitates.

"You're not going to tell her, are you?"

I leave him there. When I step into the foyer the music is going proper, really loud. The party has begun.

Fifty minutes later too much vodka is gone.

"There you are!" Chris yells. I turn really slowly and after a second the rest of the room turns with me. "I've been looking for you. Let's go outside."

"Go without me. I'm going to stay . . . here."

He grins. "Come on; the fresh air will make you feel better."

I let him drag me outside. I look up. The sun gets in my eyes.

Everything goes white.

"Oh my God, it's true."

"Go away."

I'm flat on my back. Perfectly manicured blades of grass press into my legs, hands and neck.

"The sooner you make a mistake and learn to live with it, the better. You're not responsible for everything. You can't control the way things end up."

"Evan's cheating on you with Jenny Morse. They're fucking."

All of a sudden I'm being jerked upright. My stomach lurches. I try to tell whichever one of them it is to stop and leave me alone, but I can't move my mouth.

"Parker, sit up. You can't stay on your back because if you get sick—"

"I hope she chokes."

"Nice, Evan. Would you just leave?"

"Not until you talk to me about this."

"If I talk to you about this now, I'll just say something that you really won't like—"

When I wake up, I'm still drunk.

I stumble through the kitchen, head outside and throw up in some bushes until there's nothing left in my stomach to throw up. When it's over, I spot Jessie by the pool, laughing it up with some guy I don't know. He looks older than us and she's in full party mode, probably buzzed, and the way she leans into him is wrong because it's how she leans into a guy when she wants to fuck him.

I blink. I'm on the lawn. I blink again and Jessie is making out with a new mystery guy, different from the last one. I blink again and Evan's screaming at both of them.

I blink again and I'm in front of the drinks table set out on the lawn. I go straight for the bowl of punch, fill a cup with shaking hands, drink it, then another.

Then, a voice behind me:

"Someone spiked that, like, an hour ago."

I drop the cup and moan.

"Where's Jessie?"

"She was crying her eyes out. She said she was going to run away." Becky looks up at me and smiles. "Nice going, Parker."

"Where did she go?"

Becky points in the direction of the woods.

I can't feel my feet, but I soldier on. The farther I get from the house, the louder the music sounds.

Chris's parties are the best except when they're not.

Twenty-five steps into the woods, and my head is barely attached to my neck, but there's something I have to fix, so I keep moving.

A few more steps. I hear something and I stop.

I can make out two shapes in the darkness, on the ground. On a bed of pine needles. My heart sinks. I inch forward and hold my breath.

Jessie's fucking him.

Except that's not what it is at all.

I breathe in. The air is stagnant from all the people wandering around the property dancing, drinking, smoking. These dirty scents mingle with the damp summer air and fresh-cut grass and there's Jessie and that guy, this clean-cut frat boy with an ugly mouth and dead eyes, and she's crying and it's not sex; it's a rape. He forces her to her feet and drags her away and I'm alone and then Chris is taking me back inside. And the next night I'm sick and Mrs. Wellington calls and asks us if we've seen Jessie, if she's with us, and I don't say anything and when she becomes a missing person and the police start asking questions I tell them I don't know anything and everyone vouches for me because I was drunk and stupid and when I find her bracelet in the woods two weeks later I think it's there for me because I killed her and I take it and I wear it so I never forget even though I'll never forget and I never say a word to anyone because if I hadn't said anything in the first place none of this would have—

JESSICA WELLINGTON. MISSING.

I rip the poster off the wall.

twenty-four

"I'm sorry," Jake says.

I crumple the poster, walk over to the garbage and get rid of it. If I don't get rid of it, no one will, and if no one gets rid of it—

Once my hands are empty, I don't know what to do with them, so I snap. My fingers.

"Chris said she was your—your best . . ." He trails off like the gravity of the situation has hit him full on, like he knew Jessie, and it's funny watching that happen on his face. Better his than mine. "I'm so sorry."

I tilt my chin defiantly, still snapping.

"I bet you—" I have to wait three finger snaps before I can speak. "I—"

And then I'm walking down the hall, away from him, walking down the hall as fast as I can, as close as I can get to running without actually doing it. People pass me on their way to classes or to Becky, who's always been a kind of celebrity because everyone thinks she's the last person who saw Jessie alive and Jessie told her she was running away and everything and Chris is probably holding her through it, because that's traumatizing, you know, and I feel like I'm going to throw up.

I'm really going to throw up.

I push through the back doors, outside, at the same time Henley announces a special assembly in the auditorium. I gag on the fresh air and let the thought take over: Jessie's dead Jessie's dead she's dead she's dead. I end up on my knees, but I don't vomit. I dig my fingers into the pavement until the fingernail on the index finger of my right hand snaps back and there's red.

"Shit."

I suck on my finger and taste my own blood. It hurts. I want to scream.

Instead, I get calm.

Like, leaving-my-body calm.

I stand and brush bits of gravel and dirt off my skirt and knees at the same time the doors behind me open. It's Evan. His mouth is a terrible *O* and he makes these gasping noises, fish-out-of-water sounds. He's heard.

"Jessie's dead," I tell him.

He lets out this groan, curls his hands into fists and presses them into his eyes and sobs. The calm that's enveloped me never falters. I wonder if I should be worried about this.

I should be worried about this.

"I can't believe it." He wipes his eyes with the back of his sleeve. "I can't. I—"

"You didn't actually think she was coming back?" I always make it worse. "I called it ages ago. Dead."

He chokes. "Bitch."

"Fuck you."

"Fuck you." His neck and face turn red. "Show a little respect. She did more for you than you ever did for her."

"Fuck you."

We could probably do this all day. And Jessie's dead. I pinch my arm.

"I should get back in," he finally mutters, sniffing. His eyes well up again. The closer he gets to crying, the further I feel from it myself. "Chris will be looking for me. I should go back. . . ."

"What's stopping you?"

"Becky."

"What?"

"I can't stand being around her. She—" The tears spill over. He buries his head in his hands, and if it was anyone but me next to him he'd be comforted. "I mean, I don't like you, but if you told me you were running away, I'd stop you. I'd talk you out of it. Becky didn't even . . . I mean—"

"Bullshit," I mutter. "You would've driven me home, helped me pack and given me enough bus fare to get out of town."

"So that's what you think of me. You really think I—"

He stops. He cheats on his girlfriends. He knows what I think of him.

"Why did you come back?" I ask. "Why would you come back to this when everyone thinks it's you—that you made her run—"

"Because," he says. "It's what I deserve."

I swallow. "What did she say to you?"

"What are you talking about?" He stares at me. But he knows what I'm talking about. "Why are you asking me all these—I have to . . . I have to go inside."

He brushes past me.

"At the party," I say at his back. "She said something— she said she was going to say something you wouldn't like."

"You said you didn't remember the party," he says slowly.

"Like I'd tell you otherwise." I wrap my arms around my-self. "I remember."

The parts I'd like to forget.

He faces me.

"She said she'd never forgive me and that she—" He chokes on the words. "That she hoped I was guilty for the rest of my life, but I didn't know she was planning to—I didn't—"

And he's crying again.

"Oh, give me a break, Evan," I snap, because I'm annoyed by the sound of it, the idea that he would make himself guilty because Jessie said she hoped he would be. She wasn't like that. "She wasn't that type of person and you know it. She would've forgiven you."

"But that's what she said and then she ran away so I would—"

"She was a good person."

"No," Evan says, crying even harder. "She said she would run away and she did it to get back at me—" Shut up. Shut up. *Shut up.* "But she wasn't supposed to—she said she was going to run away and now she's—"

"She didn't run away!"

His tears stop and my heart is going crazy in my chest because it wants out of me and I want out of me and I hate him, I hate Evan, I've always hated him because it's my fault he's ruined and it's all I think when I see him, it's my fault and I could fix him, but I don't want to give that to him because if I do, I have to tell and I've never told anyone *it's my fault.*

"She ran away," he says.

"She was in the woods. She was with—" I shake my head. I want it out of my head, but I don't want to say it. "No, you're right. She ran away—"

I start walking, put some distance between us. I don't even know where I'm going. He grabs me by the arm and pulls me back.

"Parker, who was she with?"

I shrug him off.

"Some guy. Leave me alone, Evan, I have to—"

"This was after Becky saw her? After she told Becky she was running away?"

"I have to go," I say, moving again, and he grabs me again. "I have things I need to—I have—"

"Parker."

I close my eyes.

"Yes."

"Who was she with?"

"I don't know."

"What happened?"

So I tell him.

"You didn't . . ." He stares at me like I'm some kind of monster.

My mouth is dry, parched. I feel slightly sick again but beyond that—nothing.

"Why?" he demands.

"I don't know. I don't—"

His hands come out and he shoves me hard and I fall back and hit the ground hard and I want to stay there, but he's on me, clawing at my arms and my shirt, anything he can get a hold on, trying to get me up again, and all I can think is *yes* and he's screaming at me, "You bitch, this is your fault, I thought it was me this whole time," and his fingernails dig into my skin and I keep saying, "I know, I know, I know," but I can't feel anything and then Chris is there and he's pushing Evan back, and he's screaming, too, "What the fuck are you doing, man? Get the fuck out of here!"

I scramble to my hands and knees, gravel digging into my skin. As soon as I'm on my feet, Evan makes another lunge at me, but Chris pushes him back.

"It was her! I thought it was me!" Evan's voice is hoarse. "It was her—"

"Get the fuck out of here, Evan!"

Chris gives Evan one last shove and Evan swears and stalks across the parking lot. There are angry red fingernail scratches up and down my arms, a little blood here and there. But it feels like nothing. Chris turns to me, furious.

"What did you say to him?" he says. "What the *fuck* did you say to him?"

"Chris," Becky says, "don't—"

And then Jake asks if I'm okay, but I shrug, shrug, shrug them all off. This is so stupid.

"Get away from me."

This is *so* stupid. I have plans and I'm not letting this ruin them because Jessie's been dead forever and I'm still alive and I still have things to do.

I head back inside, straight for my locker.

I wait for the JD to settle before I exit the stall. I wait until I know I'm good and wasted and everyone would know it to look at me, just like old times, and I walk unsteadily across the washroom floor and I fumble with the door for a minute before I pull it open and I step into the hall and crash into someone.

I hope it's Grey.

Or Henley.

twenty-five

Jack Daniel's is a more unsavory color coming up than going down—it always is—and I'm hunched over a toilet I don't recognize, puking my guts out.

I don't know where I am.

I hope I'm so wasted I can't tell I'm actually at home. After I'm done puking—it feels like forever—I float to my feet and a pair of hands guides me to a bed that swallows me alive. It's not my bed. I'm definitely not at home.

Maybe the hospital?

I inch my eyes open and the room goes in and out of focus. I catch a glimpse of a photo on the wall I've seen before. I'm at Chris's house. Saved again. But I don't want to be saved. I try to say it, but I can't get the words out of my mouth, only garbled sound. Someone says something to me in a soothing tone and I mumble something back, but I don't know what I'm saying, hearing, anything.

I don't know how to live with myself.

Even before Jessie disappeared, I never understood how I was supposed to work as a person or how I was supposed to work with other people. Something was really wrong with me, like I felt wrong all the time. I longed for some kind of symmetry, a balance. I chose perfection. Opposite of wrong. Right. Perfect. Good.

I get caught up in outcomes. I convince myself they're truths. No one will notice how wrong you are if everything you do ends up right. The rest becomes incidental. So incidental that, after a while, you forget. Maybe you are perfect. Good. It must be true. Who can argue with results? You're not so wrong after all. So you buy into it and you go crazy maintaining it. Except it creeps up on you sometimes, that you're not right. Imperfect. Bad. So you snap your fingers and it goes away.

Until something you can't ignore happens and you see it all over yourself.

And there's only one thing left to do.

I throw myself at Chris, wrap my arms around him and press my lips against his, something I haven't done in a long time. He holds on to me, surprised, and I reach into his pocket and grab his wallet. It snags on his jeans and I give it a little tug. Maybe he feels it and pretends he doesn't. Two hundred miles later, he's three hundred dollars poorer and I'm at the Morton Motel getting ready to die.

I debate leaving a note, but it comes out like a legal waiver.

I unscrew the bottle of pills and the booze, and with every bitter swallow I'm less afraid of myself. I'm finally doing the right thing. Except I fuck it up and I end up in the hospital where I get my stomach pumped and I live. The first time I wake up, I think I've died and I think it's heaven.

The second time I wake up, I know I'm in hell and Chris is crying over me.

"I can't pay you back," I murmur thickly.

"Are you awake?"

I take a deep breath in. The air is sweet, dead-flower sweet. My stomach turns and I think I'm going to throw up, but I don't. A minute later, I open my eyes. I'm in Chris's guest room and he's sitting on the bed, peering at me. The lamp on the nightstand is on, casting a weak yellow wash over both of us, and the window reveals a black night sky outside.

My head aches.

"I know that face," Chris says quietly. And then he starts explaining, like I asked, like I even care. "Becky found you, and Jake and I got you out of school by—by the grace of God, I think."

My mouth tastes vomit sour.

"Because we were looking all over for you after Evan . . ."

He edges up the bed until he's close enough to hold my hand and then he does it and I wish he wouldn't. And I wish he'd shut up.

"She's been dead awhile. Jessie." He says it like he can't believe it. His voice breaks. "I mean, a long time ago. I heard it on the news this morning, before I came to school. I guess they found her over the weekend. That was on the news, too. But they didn't say who it was because they had to . . . they had—it's crazy, isn't it? I mean, when you think about it. It doesn't feel real."

"Chris." My voice comes out splintered, gravel. "Stop talking."

"But no one thought she was alive anyway, did they."

He stares at the wall, his eyes bright. He swallows once, twice, three times, his Adam's apple going up and down. A couple tears slide down his cheek and he brushes them away.

"Jake said you told him you wanted to die." He turns to me and the look in his eyes reminds me of Bailey on the side of the road. "I went downstairs to get water and you told him you wanted to die."

"Anyone would say that after a bottle of Jack Daniel's," I say.

"That's not how you meant it and you know it." He keeps looking at me until I'm the one who has to look away. "Why?"

I want to sit up, but I can't guarantee my stomach won't revolt and it's a miracle I haven't already puked on the white duvet.

"I want to die, I guess."

It gets so quiet.

"Why?"

But I've had enough. He wasn't even supposed to find me. Henley, Grey—*they* were supposed to find me and kick me out of school so my parents would give up on me and then everyone would give up on me and I wouldn't have to worry anymore. I push the duvet off, swing my legs over the bed and stand.

"I'm going," I tell him.

"Parker—"

My legs are shaky, but I make it across the room and then I get to the door and I puke. I mean, I feel it coming up, clamp my hand over my mouth and reach the bathroom just in time. My stomach muscles scream. A few dry heaves later, I'm propped up against the wall, panting. I rest my head against my knees while Chris stands in the doorway, watching. A bead of sweat trickles down the back of my neck and under my shirt collar. I gulp air like it's going out of style.

"You think I ever stopped wanting to die after the motel?" I ask. "You think a feeling like that just goes away?"

He steps forward and steels himself like he's about to give a speech to a room full of people. He probably thought one up the whole time I was out, just waiting for me to wake up

so he could say it and we could have A Moment That Would
Turn It All Around. But if you learn anything by the time
you're eighteen, it's that those moments don't happen in real
life. Ever.

"I don't want you to die," he says woodenly, but the funny
thing is, he really means it. "I don't want to go to your memorial service."

"Memorial service," I repeat. "When's Jessie's memorial
service going to be?"

"Are you even listening to me?"

I groan, rest my head against the wall and close my eyes.

"I'm just tired, Chris. And my stomach hurts and I have
a headache and—" My voice breaks. She's dead and I am not
going to cry. "I'm tired."

"Then you should sleep," he says.

I find my way to my feet and head back to the bedroom.
Chris follows close behind. I crawl under the covers and he
pulls the duvet up around me.

"It shouldn't be like this for you," he says. "You need
help."

"What I need is for everyone to leave me alone. That's
what I want."

"Parker, you don't want that. Everyone's on to you and
you don't even know it. You have to stop this; you have to—"
I think he's crying. "I don't want you to die."

I roll over so my back is to him.

"It's just Jessie," I say into the pillow. "I'm just shocked
about it. That's all."

But the truth is, I haven't felt a thing since Evan.

"Yeah, but you've always needed help," Chris points out.
"Even she knew it. I think she'd want that for you."

"And I don't think we should be talking about me."

I close my eyes.

twenty-six

"How are you doing?"

It's not like when someone who's there one minute is gone the next.

It's worse.

"I'm great."

"So," Jake says, staring at me expectantly. "Are we going to stand in front of the school all day or are we going in?"

I stare up at the concrete building. The memorial service is today.

"You could always go in without me," I tell him. Before he can say anything, I ask, "Do you think if I'd told you it would've made a difference? About how I knew Jessie?"

"Between us?" he asks. I nod. "Probably not, unless you had a completely different personality or something. But then I doubt I'd have found you as interesting."

"Sounds like I was destined to screw you over, then."

"Doesn't it."

At least I didn't have to stress over what I was going to wear to the service. Thank God for school uniforms, just this once. But I couldn't find my dress shoes, so I'm wearing muddy running shoes. And I forgot to brush my hair.

"Too bad it couldn't have been different."

He shrugs. "It can always be different."

It's weird the way all of this has dulled the fact we had sex and I ran. My parents have forgotten about Bailey. Henley and Grey don't care about me skipping afternoon classes. It's okay I spent the night at Chris's. It's okay because Jessie's dead.

Because they don't know what I did. Didn't do.

"Are you ready to go in?" Jake asks.

"I can't go in."

"Chris will be there and I'll be there." He clears his throat. "Uh . . . and Becky will be there, too."

"Well, if *Becky's* going to be there . . ."

A few cars pull into the parking lot. I recognize Mr. and Mrs. Wellington's Saab right away. My chest tightens.

"I can't go in," I repeat. I snap my fingers. "Make an excuse for me. Please."

"I can do that for you," he says. I must sound desperate enough. He pauses. "What was she like?"

My stomach ties itself into little knots and I keep snapping my fingers.

"You have this knack for asking questions I don't want to answer."

"You don't have to answer it."

"She was like . . ." I raise my head and look to the sky and try to think of a way to put it. "She was like a buffer between me and the rest of the world. Nice. Good."

He reaches out and gives my shoulder a squeeze before heading into the school without me.

After a while, Evan shows up.

Or maybe he's always been there, watching from his car in the parking lot or behind the sole maple tree they planted in front of the school to make it look less like a concrete penitentiary; I don't know. He's just here, which means I have to leave.

I hurry up the steps, wrench the front door open and—

Except I can't go inside.

"I just want to talk," he says.

"Is that all? Sure you don't want to attack me again, too?"

He sighs.

"I shouldn't have done that. I—"

"Evan, I don't care."

"Oh, right, I get it," he says. "You're right back into it, aren't you?"

"Back into what?"

The wind picks up, pushing my hair in my face. I shiver, brush it away and face him. I try to read what's in his eyes, but there's nothing there. I remember when I caught him with Jenny. How scared he was. And I was happy because I wanted to hurt Jessie for caring that I spent junior year hiding out in the girls' room between periods, hyperventilating. She wanted to help me and I wanted to hurt her for it because I didn't want anyone to know because it was important because . . .

Perfect people don't break.

I can't remember what was running through me when I saw her face pressed into the ground with that guy on top of her, I was so out of it, but I can't convince myself it wasn't bad. All I know is I went to a party and I was the catalyst for every horrible thing that happened there and after and I don't know why I didn't say anything when I saw her and I don't know why I didn't say anything later and I don't know how to fix it and I'm afraid of what happens next, so I have to keep doing it this way until it's right again, but I don't know how to make it right again because I'm always wrong.

I'm a bad person.

"You'll just go on until the next party," Evan says.

"Fuck you."

I'd rather be in school. I turn around and open the door, but I can't go in.

"It wouldn't have made a difference."

The handle slips from my grasp and the door clicks closed. "What?"

I face him slowly because I'm afraid of what he said. What I think he said.

"I run it through my head every single fucking day, trying to figure it out—and there was a . . ." He pauses. "There was a group of college guys; they crashed it. And Jessie was all over them to get back at me. And I . . . I was there when Chris carried you out of the woods, after you must've . . . after you saw it happen and you were . . . you—"

He shakes his head and squints up at me.

"You couldn't have changed anything."

"You don't know that."

He makes a face like he wants to hit something or scream. And then it disappears and he's just tired looking, old. But I still don't believe him.

"They're pretty sure she was dead before the night was out." He clenches his hands. "And I *wish* it was your fault. If I could make it your fault, I would."

"It is. If she hadn't known about you—and I let everyone think she ran away—"

"You should've told," he agrees. "But it wouldn't have made a difference."

"Why are you telling me this?"

"Because last night I was thinking about it and I just knew—" And then he starts crying. God, he's always crying. "That she wanted me to."

I bring a shaking hand to my eyes.

"You can't know that," I tell him. "You're wrong."

This strange and horrible feeling takes up residence in the middle of my chest and spreads through the rest of my body. Something insides me caves and I'm afraid this is going to be the panic attack that kills me.

The one where my heart beats so fast it disintegrates.

I pull open the door and stumble into the school and I think he calls me back, Evan, but I don't care. I walk past the doors to the auditorium; I'm walking blind and everything hurts. I want to cry, it hurts so bad, but I promised myself I wouldn't cry because I don't deserve to cry over her. And I want to believe what he's saying is true, but no one can say it's true and it doesn't matter because it doesn't *change* anything because she's dead and she's never coming back and it's my fault and I miss her, *I miss her so much*. I can't breathe. I can't. I reach out for the wall and force myself to keep moving because I hear voices coming from the auditorium. It's over. The service is over.

So I have to get away.

Walk, Parker; just keep walking. Just keep—

"Parker?"

I blink.

I'm looking into a sparrow's dead eyes.

And then I look at my hands. I'm sitting on the floor and there's a crowd. And then I spot Bailey in the back and he's staring and he looks sad, but I don't—

"Parker?" the sparrow says gently. "Parker, can you hear me?"

I don't want to do this anymore, but I don't know what else to do.

I've never done it any other way.

twenty-seven

"Clearing out, huh?"

Chris and Becky walk up to me, holding hands. If the events of the last few weeks have done anything, they've made them a stronger couple. So strong, in fact, it doesn't really matter they have nothing in common because they're really, really serious about each other now. I wasn't there when it happened, but I think it means he's over me.

I reach into my locker, pull out all of my books and set them on the floor next to the garbage bag beside me. I don't know how such a small rectangle of space could hold so much crap, but there it is.

"Yep," I say. Wedged in the very back of the top shelf is a T-shirt I thought I'd lost ages ago. I toss it into the garbage bag.

"Will you have to repeat the year?" Becky asks.

"Would that make you happy?"

"I just wondered."

"Grey and Henley are working something out. I'll be

graduating; I just won't be . . ." I toss a few crumpled pieces of paper into the garbage. "I just won't be here."

"I'll miss you," Chris says.

My locker is empty. They didn't want me to come back and empty it, but I insisted. I didn't want anyone else touching my things. I tie up the garbage bag and brush my hands on my jeans.

"It's not like I won't still live two streets away," I tell him.

"Yeah, I know," he says. "I just thought it was worth saying."

So this is it. These things happen fast, I guess. From the moment in the hall to telling Grey the truth to her creaming herself and telling my parents to them crying to the news slowly traveling through the school and not everyone thinks it's my fault, but no one can say anything for sure. And I'm supposed to know what to do with that. Just like that. The Jessica Wellington murder is all over the local news and sometimes I make myself watch it for hours. They're calling it a kind of nervous breakdown. I don't know. I've had a couple appointments with that shrink. It was okay.

"Big game against St. Anthony's next weekend," Becky says tensely, changing the subject. There's something validating about the fact she still sees me as a threat, even like this.

"Decide on the cheer?" I ask.

"Not yet."

"Do the 'win, lose, it's all the same' one."

Her eyes light up. "You think?"

I nod. "I think."

She studies me. "You're not serious."

"I am," I insist. "I'd even come to the game just to watch everyone laugh at you."

She turns pink.

"Maybe you should see if they can't do something about your personality when they're fixing your brain," she snaps.

"Anyway," Chris says quickly. He gives me a hug. "We've got to go. We're meeting Evan for lunch. You need a ride or anything?"

"My mom's picking me up." I give him a small squeeze back. "But you can do me a favor and toss the garbage in the Dumpster outside."

"Sure." He hesitates, like he wants to say something else but doesn't know how to say it. Then he brings his mouth close to my ear and murmurs quietly enough so Becky can't hear, "I love you."

But it's different now.

"I'm sorry," I say.

"I know. I knew it before you did."

He leans back and smiles at me while Becky scratches her head, oblivious to the whole exchange. And she's going to live out the rest of her life like that, but good for her. Chris picks up the garbage bag and swings it over his shoulder.

"Jake's around here somewhere," he says.

"How about that."

I bend down, gather my books and shove them into my bag.

"See you, Parker," Becky says.

"You can call anytime," Chris says over his shoulder. Becky holds out her hand and he takes it. "If you want."

I wait until they're gone before I heave my book bag onto my shoulders and straighten up, the bones in my arms and legs crackling in protest. I make the slow trek down the hall. The lunch bell rang twenty minutes ago and it's mostly quiet but for the distant sounds of talking and laughter coming from the cafeteria.

I run into Jake outside of art. He's leaning against the door, his arms crossed.

"Hey . . . hey, you—girl," he says.

It almost makes me smile, but I can't. "Hey . . . hey, you—New Kid."

"You're really leaving?"

I nod and adjust my book bag.

"Yeah. I'm going to get my head screwed on straight and everything. Figure out what's . . ." Even now, I hate saying it. "What's been wrong with me."

"Good," he says. "Is this what you want?"

"I think so."

He lets his arms fall to his sides. "I'm glad."

"I hear admitting you have a problem is half the battle."

He stares at me expectantly. I should apologize to him.

"Are you going to be around this summer?" I ask instead.

"Nope," he says.

"Why?" I hope it wasn't me. I know it was me. "I mean, it's none of my business. But I bet whatever you're doing can't be more exciting than the therapy sessions I'll be stuck in."

"Probably not," Jake agrees. "I'll be at my mom's."

My mouth drops open and he nods.

"Yeah, I know." He gives me a lopsided grin. "She doesn't want me to come, but I'm coming. Dad figures she'll let me in if I show up on her doorstep and if not, he'll foot the plane ticket back here. We'll see what happens."

"Wow."

"It was you," he says. "I wouldn't have done it, but after we . . ."

It hangs in the air between us. I swallow.

"And after summer it's straight to college, right?"

"Taking the year off, actually," Jake says.

"Oh," I say, surprised. "And then you're coming back here?"

"Yep."

"And I'll be here." As soon as it's off my lips I'm sorry

I've said it. I'm just pushing my luck and I don't even know why. There's nothing to push. It's over. I clear my throat. "Anyway, good luck with your mom."

"Good luck to you, too," he says.

That's my cue to go, but my feet are cemented to the floor. He waits for me to move and I can't because I want everything taken care of before I can start taking care of everything. I know that's not the way life happens. There are no tidy resolutions. Ask me if I think it was my fault, if I think this heaviness will ever go away.

"I'm scared," I admit.

"That's because it's scary," he says. "But it'll be better this way."

If he says so, it must be true.

"I jerked you around," I blurt out. "I didn't give you a chance."

"Yeah," he says. "I know."

And it's awkward and I hate it, but I have to accept it because I'm supposed to be accepting things now and working with what's left. Because that's what my psychiatrist told me to do. So I almost hold out my hand to shake his, a symbol of acceptance and moving on, but even I'm smart enough to know how stupid that would be.

So I force a smile at him and continue my way down the hall.

"Hey, Parker?"

I pause.

"I'll see you in the fall," he says. "I mean, you never know, right? Maybe we'll actually get somewhere this time."

I turn around and he's standing in the middle of the hall, smiling at me, but I can't think of anything to say. We stay like that for a minute until he inclines his head and goes where he's going and I'm alone, like I've wanted forever, except that's not really true because Mom's waiting for me outside and there's a shrink waiting for me in the city and there's nothing I can do about the past.

"Recovery" is going to be boring and painful and painfully boring, I can already tell. Which is good, I guess.

I hope it works.

Megan Gunter

Courtney Summers lives and writes in Canada. She is the author of several critically acclaimed novels for young adults, including *Cracked Up to Be, Some Girls Are, Fall for Anything, This Is Not a Test, All the Rage,* and most recently, *Sadie,* a *New York Times* bestseller, Indie bestseller, Odyssey Award winner, Audie Award Winner, and Edgar Award nominee, appearing on more than thirty Best Of lists in 2018. Learn more at courtneysummers.ca.